W9-DCZ-229

The Campfire Girls as Federal Investigators

The Camp Fire Girls as Federal Investigators

By JULIANNE DEVRIES

The World Syndicate Publishing Co.

CLEVELAND, OHIO NEW YORK

Printed in the United States of America

PART I

As Federal Investigators

CHAPTER I

The first warm days of spring were clearing the streets of the little town of Oakdale of the last signs of winter. The sun shone brightly, the birds sang and all about were signs of new life and joy of living but in the heart of pretty, vivacious, red haired Lenore Rivers was naught but gloom.

Returning the day before from the first spring meeting of Wa-Wan-Da Camp Fire of which she was a member, Lenore had spied a hat in a shop window. It was a very pretty hat, saucy and pert, an exact duplication of the style of the moment. A jaunty feather added just the right touch of color and as Lenore stopped to admire the creation, she thought how well that particular hat would set off her flaming red hair. Suddenly her eyes opened wide and she stared hard, scarcely daring to believe what she saw. At the base of the little stand atop which the hat was perched was a small card and on that card was printed a numeral that Lenore could not believe was true.

"They must have made a mistake," she murmured to herself, "a hat like that couldn't possibly sell for so little. Why, they're giving it away at that price!"

And in order to satisfy her curiosity, Lenore entered the shop. Some minutes later she emerged from the store, a happy smile on her face and a new hat on her head. That, however, was yesterday. On her way home from school the following afternoon, a sudden spring shower sent Lenore, wearing her new hat, scurrying for the nearest doorway. The rain ceased as abruptly as it had begun and as the sun peeped out from behind the vanishing clouds, Lenore continued on her way home.

As she walked, she became dimly conscious of a growing sensation of tightness around her head and she began to wonder why people who passed her on the street looked suddenly alarmed. Turning a corner, Lenore saw two familiar figures approaching whom she recognized as portly Mabel Chapman and petite, blonde Alice Blake, members with her in Wa-Wan-Da Camp Fire, as were tall and graceful Dolores Rodriguez and black haired, merry Anita Brooks, both of whom appeared on the front porch of Dolores' home a second later. As the four girls diminished the distance between themselves and Lenore, they suddenly stopped in astonishment and then, with one accord, burst into peals of merry laughter. Perplexed, Lenore looked about her to discover the cause of her friends' merriment but seeing nothing, she walked on.

"Oh," gasped Anita, leaning against a tree for support, "I never saw anything so funny in all my life! Why didn't you tell us you'd joined a circus, Lenore?"

"Maybe she's advertising something," giggled Mabel, "and people are supposed to follow her to the place she's working for! Tell us about it, Lenore, please!"

"I don't know what you mean," replied Lenore indignantly, "unless you're all jealous of my new hat! I bought it yesterday at Wilson's. Like it?"

Far from silencing her friends' ridicule, however, Lenore's remark brought forth fresh gales of laughter. Incensed, Lenore was about to continue on her way when Dolores caught her by the coat sleeve and pulled her back toward her house.

"Come inside a minute," she laughed, "I want to show you something interesting."

"Very interesting," chuckled Alice as she and the others followed Lenore and Dolores into the latter's house. "In fact it's the most interesting thing yet!"

Propelling the bewildered Lenore up the stairs while the others trooped behind, Dolores pushed open the door of her bedroom and pointed to the large mirror over her dressing table. Halfway across the room, Lenore caught her reflection in the glass and with a startled cry, ran to the mirror and stared unbelievingly at what she saw there while the rest of the girls watched in amusement.

Staring back at her from the mirror, Lenore saw a face, undeniably her face but one that was streaked with a variety of colors ranging in shades from blue to red while on top of her head, was a small, sodden lump that had once been a hat.

"My new hat!" wailed Lenore, snatching the sorry thing from her head, "and look at my face! I'll never be able to wash that dye off and I'll never dare go out on the streets again! The whole town must have seen me looking like this!"

Several days later, Mr. Charles Downie, president of the Oakdale Chamber of Commerce looked up from a letter he was reading and cleared his throat. Peering over his spectacles at his secretary who sat across the desk from him, he handed her the letter and waited until she had finished reading it before he spoke.

"Get Mrs. Evans on the phone," commanded Mr. Downie as his secretary handed back the letter. "I don't know what she can do about it but a request from the United States Department of Customs can't be ignored. Ask her to come down here."

Half an hour later, young and pretty Florence Evans, leader and Guardian of Wa-Wan-Da Camp Fire of Oakdale was sitting in Mr. Downie's office, reading the letter. The missive, addressed to the president of the Oakdale Chamber of Commerce, informed him of the fact that, as president of the Chamber of Commerce, it was his duty to warn all shopkeepers of his town against purchasing unusually low priced goods. Such goods, the letter went on, were of an inferior quality and were undoubtedly being smuggled into the country, although no actual proof of that fact existed. As the puzzled Camp Fire leader read the letter, she was at a loss as to why Mr. Downie had asked her to his office and why she had been given that letter to read. The solution to her perplexity, however, was contained in the last paragraph.

"We ask, therefore, (she read) that you communicate at once with Mrs. Florence Evans of your city and acquaint her with the contents of this letter, since, for obvious reasons, this department cannot establish direct contact with her. Please inform Mrs. Evans that we are anxious to obtain her services as well as those of the five young ladies, all of whom have rendered such invaluable assistance to the government in the past. Kindly ascertain if Mrs. Evans and the Misses Dolores Rodriguez, Mabel Chapman, Anita Brooks, Alice Blake and Lenore Rivers are at liberty to accept an assignment from this department and advise us at once. (signed) B. W. Hill."

Smiling, Mrs. Evans gave the letter back to Mr. Downie and rose from her chair.

"I had no idea you and your Camp Fire girls were so important," remarked Mr. Downie, rising with Mrs. Evans. "What do you want me to do about that letter?"

"I know there isn't any need to consult the girls," replied Mrs. Evans, still smiling. "I can speak for them as well as myself. When you answer Mr. Hill's letter, tell him we gladly accept and are awaiting his further instructions."

As she left the building, a hasty glance at her watch told the Camp Fire leader that scarcely an hour remained before school would be over for the day. Opening the door of her automobile, she got in and as she started the motor, an idea suddenly occurred to her and so, instead of going home as she originally intended, the Camp Fire leader swung her machine around and drove to the large, red brick high school building where the five girls were pupils. The letter she had just read in Mr. Downie's office meant the temporary abandonment of school activities for five girls and Mrs. Evans was beginning to be worried.

Early last winter the schools of Oakdale were forced to close because of an influenza epidemic and coincidental with the closing had come a summons from the United States Department of Justice, sending the girls and Mrs. Evans on a secret mission across the country to California. Their work in behalf of the government and their subsequent visit to friends in Washington had taken more time than had been planned and when the five Camp Fire girls and their pretty, young leader returned to Oakdale shortly before Christmas, they found that the school had re-opened some weeks ago. By dint of much hard study, however, the girls were soon able to catch up with their classmates but now, as Mrs. Evans entered the office of the principal, she wondered if he would permit her to withdraw the girls from school again.

Kindly, old Henry Masson, who had been principal of Oakdale High school almost as long as anyone could remember, greeted Mrs. Evans with his usual jovial cordiality and warm, boyish smile.

"This is a pleasant surprise," he beamed. "I'm glad you haven't forgotten an old man."

"Mr. Masson," began Mrs. Evans, coming directly to the point, "I'm afraid you're going to scold me but I've come to tell you that I'd like to take my girls out of school again. You know the ones I mean, Mabel Chapman, Alice Blake, Dolores Rodriguez, Anita Brooks and Lenore Rivers. The government wants us to work for them again."

"Splendid!" cried the principal in genuine enthusiasm. "Excellent! By all means, go. Oakdale High as well as myself are proud of you and those girls, Florence, and as for the school work, their records show that they are more than capable of making up whatever time is lost. Besides, just between you and I, my private opinion is that a few weeks of travel is worth more than a semester of school work. Shall I send for them now? I'd like to see their faces when you tell them about it."

"Well," laughed Mrs. Evans, "there isn't much to tell except what I've told you. I'm waiting for further details myself and if we tell the girls now, and have to wait until we receive word from Washington, they'll give the town nervous exhaustion."

Mrs. Evans did not have long to wait, however. A few days later Mr. Downie again summoned her to his office and upon her arrival there, he handed her a large, fat, sealed envelope, addressed to her, from the United States Department of Customs. Hastily tearing open the envelope, Mrs. Evans extracted a mass of papers, among which she recognized a letter addressed to her. The rest were legal documents. Unfolding the letter, her eyes grew wide as she absorbed its contents.

"Dear Mrs. Evans, (she read) the enclosed documents are, we believe, self-explanatory. They confer upon you and the Misses Dolores Rodriguez, Mabel Chapman, Alice Blake, Lenore Rivers and Anita Brooks, full authority and power to act as Federal Investigators on behalf of the Government of the United States of America, Department of Customs. Because of your excellent record of achievements in the past, we are asking you to assist us in apprehending a band of men who are flooding this country with cheap and inferior merchandise. From what our agents have been able to determine, these goods are probably being smuggled into the country at some point along the Atlantic seaboard near New York. We suggest that you and your party entrain for New York City at once or as soon as conveniently possible and report to Mr. James H. Baldwin, Deputy Collector of Customs of the Port of New York who will instruct you further. Attached to each of the six documents enclosed herewith, you will find Federal railway passes, entitling those to whom they are issued to free transportation on any railroad in the country. Please wire this office advising the exact time of your departure from Oakdale so that we may act accordingly. Please know that the full resources of this department will be at your entire disposal at all times. (signed)

B. W. Hill."

As soon as she finished reading the letter, the thrilled Camp Fire Guardian dashed from the office of the startled Mr. Downie, calling a hasty farewell as she ran. Reaching her home, Mrs. Evans, still clutching the precious documents in her hand, telephoned first one and then another of the five Camp Fire girls, instructing them to come to her house at once with their parents. Next the busy woman phoned her husband at his office and then she called the ticket office at the railroad station to acquaint herself with the time of certain train schedules. She was still talking to the station master at the depot when Billy Evans, her husband came dashing into the house, breathless and wild eyed for his excited wife had forgotten to tell him why she wanted him to come home in such a hurry. Fearful lest some accident had occurred, Mr. Evans had sped from his law office, with such haste that Police Sergeant Blake, Alice's father, seeing him, had chased after him. Both men arrived at the house almost simultaneously, Mr. Evans wide eyed with alarm and Sergeant Blake on the alert for any possible disturbance.

"What's the matter, Flo?" cried the breathless Mr. Evans. "What happened? Tell me!"

"Why nothing, Billy," replied Mrs. Evans, startled at her husband's appearance and the presence of Sergeant Blake, "except that I have wonderful news. What's the matter with you? You look as though you had seen a ghost or something."

And as Mrs. Evans proceeded to tell her husband

and Sergeant Blake of the letter she had received a short while ago, Mr. Evans collapsed into a chair with a sigh of relief while Sergeant Blake threw back his head and roared with laughter.

"You should have seen him run!" laughed the sergeant. "I thought something serious had happened and took after him. Well, you don't need me, so I'll be on my way."

"But we do need you!" protested Mrs. Evans. "I just phoned all the girls to come over with their parents. Alice and her mother will be here in a moment. You see, we'll have to go to New York and I want you and Billy to help me convince the others that it will be all right to let the girls go. You've done it before, you know."

Sergeant Blake's powers of persuasion were not needed as much that afternoon as they had been in the past, however. The parents of the five Camp Fire girls were becoming used to letting their daughters embark on strange adventures and so, after Mrs. Evans had read aloud the letter she had received that afternoon and explained to the assembled parents and the delighted and thrilled girls the nature of their new undertaking, parental permission was granted and it was agreed to start at once. The station master had informed Mrs. Evans that a train for New York would leave the Oakdale station at ten o'clock that night and it was decided that inasmuch as it would arrive at New York at noon the next day, to take it. As the happy girls left Mrs. Evans' house some time later, a grim expression crossed Lenore's usually smiling features, for she had suddenly remembered something.

"Here's where I get even for that hat!" she exclaimed determinedly.

"Was your face red!" laughed Anita as the girls walked down the street.

"And every other color too," giggled Mabel. "You looked like a blues song sounds."

"How long," demanded Lenore, "does it take to get to New York from here?"

CHAPTER II

The five Camp Fire girls could hardly wait until supper was over that night before they started to pack but at length all was in readiness and as the little group gathered at the railroad station to wait for the ten o'clock train, they excitedly discussed the adventure before them. Mabel, Dolores, Anita, Lenore and Alice, together with their young and vivacious leader, Mrs. Evans, had flown around the world and had visited many places in the United States during their adventures but of all the places they had been, New York was the favorite. Delighted at the prospect of re-visiting the great metropolis again, for they had been there before as guests of Hannah Rosenfeld, secretary of the National Camp Fire Organization, the girls were already planning shopping tours to be squeezed in somehow with their new duties as Federal Investigators.

The thundering arrival of the train put an end to further conjectures and as the girls climbed aboard, they waved farewell to those on the platform who had come to bid them goodbye. As the train roared away through the darkness, a porter conducted Mrs. Evans and the girls to the two private compartments that their Federal passes entitled them to. Finding their folding beds with which the compartments were equipped, already made up and ready for occupancy, Mrs. Evans suggested that they go to bed at once since the hour was already late and the morrow would probably make great demands on their energies.

"I'm too excited to sleep," confessed Lenore as the others began undressing. "All I can think of is what I'm going to do to those brigands in return for my hat."

"Well, go to bed anyway," advised Mrs. Evans, smiling. "I've heard it said that most well laid plots are hatched in the dark when others are fast asleep."

"In that case," asserted Mabel, "she sleeps alone. I was going to sleep with her but if she begins plotting, she's liable to dream I'm one of the smugglers and throw me out of the window or something. There's no telling what a red head will do."

"Well," giggled Anita, "if she can throw a heavyweight like you out of the window, the rest of us might as well go back to Oakdale and let the mighty Lenore handle this assignment alone. If she kicks you out of bed, Mabel, come into my compartment and I'll pick you up. I'm tired. Wake me up, somebody, when we get to New York."

Soon the two compartments were in darkness and as the five Camp Fire girls and their leader slept peacefully in their comfortable beds, the train sped on, carrying them nearer and nearer their goal and the adventure that lay before them.

Arriving in New York just as the hands of the large clocks on the walls of the Grand Central station pointed to twelve noon, the girls and Mrs. Evans hailed a cab and a few minutes later were weaving in and out of the confusing stream of traffic on their way to the lower end of Manhattan and the Customs House. Driving down Broadway, the girls gazed with delight at the crowds and tall buildings and thrilled at the activity going on all around them. Reaching lower Broadway, the cab circled little Bowling Green park and came to a halt in front of the large, grey stone building that was the Customs House. Looking diagonally across the street as they alighted from the cab, the girls saw Battery Park and the Aquarium with the Statue of Liberty faintly discernible in the distance.

Paying the cab driver, Mrs. Evans led the girls up the broad stone steps in front of the building to the lobby where a guard directed them to the office of the Deputy Collector of Customs. Although several people were waiting to see Mr. Baldwin when Mrs. Evans and the girls arrived at his office, they were ushered into his private office as soon as the girl at the switchboard informed him of their presence. Entering the room, the girls and Mrs. Evans were surprised to find that Mr. Baldwin, the Deputy Collector of Customs for the Port of New York was a rather young and handsome gentleman, instead of the elderly man they somehow had expected to see. Rising and smiling as the six newly appointed Federal Investigators walked in, Mr. Baldwin held out his hand in welcome and introduced himself to Mrs. Evans and the five girls.

"I'm James Baldwin," he smiled, "there's no use in telling you that, however. You know who I am otherwise you wouldn't be here. Now then, I know your names, too, but I'm afraid you'll have to tell me which is which. And by the way, if you'll give me your papers, I'll sign them now and then we'll go get some lunch. I'm starved."

"So am I," replied Mabel. "I'm Mabel Chapman," she continued, handing Mr. Baldwin her certificate of appointment to be signed and stamped with an official seal.

"And she's always hungry," added Anita. "You won't have any difficulty remembering her. My name is Anita Brooks," she concluded simply as one by one the girls and Mrs. Evans laid their documents before Mr. Baldwin and introduced themselves. As Mr. Baldwin affixed his signature to and stamped the last of the six certificates, he rose, the girls and Mrs. Evans rising also and picking up their bags with them.

"Why drag those heavy things around with you?" he asked. "Leave them here. We're coming back after lunch to talk business. Come on, there's a good restaurant on Pine street, just a few blocks from here off Broadway. You've never tasted anything as delicious as their cuisine. They're known all over the country for it."

"I don't care what it is," replied Mabel as the group walked up Broadway, "as long as it's edible and they give me enough of it. I'm so hungry, I could eat a horse."

As she spoke, Mabel indicated a police horse that had been walking abreast of the little party along the curb. Hearing her announcement, the policeman astride the animal gave his reins a deft jerk, sending his mount skittering away from the curb. The horse's sudden and apparent alarm over Mabel's statement brought gales of laughter from the group and the policeman, leaning down from his steed, grinned.

"Have a heart, lady," he told the embarrassed Mabel, "me and this horse has been pals for years and I couldn't bear to part with him now. Wouldn't a cow do?"

Still laughing and teasing Mabel, the girls and Mrs. Evans arrived at the corner of Wall street and Broadway. Pointing across the street, Mr. Baldwin indicated the somber structure of Trinity church and the ancient tombstones leaning crazily against each other around it. Some of them, he explained, were almost as old as the city itself. The remains of such outstanding figures in the country's history as Robert Fulton, the inventor of the steamboat, were interred there and Mr. Baldwin promised the interested girls a visit to the little cemetery on their way back.

The restaurant on Pine street, which was just a block from Wall street, to which Mr. Baldwin took Mrs. Evans and the girls, was one frequented by financial and business leaders who had their offices in the famous stock market district and while they waited for their orders to be served, Mr. Baldwin pointed out to the awed girls, various industrial leaders of the nation who were occupying tables near by. During the course of the meal, Mr. Baldwin entertained the girls and Mrs. Evans with anecdotes of New York and the famous personages residing therein until Dolores, unable to restrain her curiosity any longer, interrupted him with a question.

"But what about us?" she asked. "When, who and what are we to investigate? Are we to remain in New York? I'm dying of curiosity. Please tell us what we're to do!"

"Patience," smiled Mr. Baldwin. "I'll tell you all about it as soon as we get back to my office. In the first place, this is hardly the appropriate setting in which to discuss such things and in the second place, Mabel will tell you that dining is a pleasure and business and pleasure don't mix."

"They do with Mabel, though," giggled Lenore. "Eating is both a business and a pleasure with her and she's always pleasantly engaged in business!"

After lunch, which the girls and Mrs. Evans praised for its deliciousness, Mr. Baldwin was about to keep his promise and conduct his guests through the famous old graveyard of Trinity church when a man entered the restaurant just as he and the girls were leaving. Beckoning to Mr. Baldwin, the man spoke swiftly in a low tone and then listened while the Deputy Collector of Customs gave him hurried instructions. As the man left, Mr. Baldwin turned to Mrs. Evans and the girls.

"I'm sorry, girls," he informed them, "but there'll be no sightseeing today. That man is from my office and what he just told me makes it imperative that you get on the job at once. I was hoping to be able to entertain you for a few days before you started on your assignment but what Tommy just told me makes it necessary that not a moment be lost. We can't even spare the time to go back to the office for your bags. I'll have them sent out to where you're going. We'll take the subway, it's quicker than a cab. If we hurry, we can catch the two o'clock train. Come on!"

"But where are we going and what are we supposed to do when we get there?" asked the puzzled Camp Fire leader as Mr. Baldwin led the girls across Broadway to Rector street and down a flight of stairs to the subway station. At that hour of the day, the subway trains were almost deserted but Mr. Baldwin wished to take no chances on being overheard as he gave Mrs. Evans and the girls their instructions. Leading them to an empty car as the train came to a halt at the station, he waited until the roar of the train as it rushed through the darkness almost drowned out his words before he started to speak. Mrs. Evans and the girls had to lean forward in their seats in order to hear him as he outlined their duties.

"Now listen carefully," he began. "We're going out to Long Island. You're going to live in a house there and to all intents and purposes, I'm the real estate agent who is going to rent it to you. This house once belonged to a very rich man but has been empty for years. A caretaker and his wife live there now and you're to ask them to stay on and cook and run the place for you. You already know about the smuggling that's going on. Your job will be to investigate how and through what channels the contraband goods is being brought in here. For a while we were in the dark as to just where the stuff was being landed. We knew it was near New York some place because the city is full of it. Tommy, however, just told me that some of our men found out that the smuggler's base of operations is some place near the house you are to occupy. Now then, if we sent our men out there to investigate further, the smugglers would become suspicious and transfer their operations elsewhere but with you living under their very noses, so to speak, they'll go right on and you can catch them with the goods. As soon as you have any definite information, notify me and my office will do the rest. The house you are to live in is large and has its own private grounds, so nobody will bother you. The caretaker and his wife will do all your shopping and other errands so there will be absolutely nothing for you to do but keep your eyes and ears open. The house, fortunately, is on a hill, overlooking Long Island Sound. You'll be able to watch all boats coming into the sound and before we take the Long Island train, I'll stop at an optical goods shop and get each one of you a pair of powerful binoculars. That's all I have to tell you. The rest is up to you. As Federal Investigators, you are to act according to your own best judgment and discretion at all times."

As the girls and Mrs. Evans nodded their understanding of Mr. Baldwin's instructions, the train came to a stop at a station and two men, each bearing a heavy bundle, entered the car. Depositing their packages on empty seats, the men sat down across the aisle from Mr. Baldwin, Mrs. Evans and the girls and began to converse in a foreign tongue. At the next subway station at which the train halted, Mr. Baldwin arose and beckoning to Mrs. Evans and the girls, stepped out onto the station platform. Signs painted on the walls and attached to pillars informed Mrs. Evans and the girls that they were in the Times Square station and as he led them to an escalator at one end of the station, Mr. Baldwin grinned suddenly.

"I'm going to do something," he told the girls as they rode to an upper level, "that can't be done in any other city in the country. I'm going shopping right here underground and step from the shop into a subway train. I can make my purchase while waiting for the next train and not lose a second. We're going to buy those binoculars right here in the subway station and if you happen to need anything else, from hairpins to a dress, you can get it without bothering to go outside."

Leaving the escalator, Mr. Baldwin conducted the girls and Mrs. Evans along the upper subway level to a row of shops and while he made his purchase, Dolores, standing next to Mrs. Evans at the glass show case inside the shop, saw a reflection in a mirror on the wall opposite her that caused her to whirl around but the figures she had seen had already disappeared into the surging crowds. Mrs. Evans, however, noticed Dolores' action and putting down the binoculars she was examining, asked her what she had seen that caused her such sudden alarm. Dolores, however, shook her head and smiled sheepishly. The others were engrossed in peering through the various glasses the shop keeper brought them and had not seen Dolores' move.

"I'm getting jumpy, I guess," the Camp Fire girl confessed to her leader. "I just saw those two men with the bundles that got on the subway train just before we got off, only this time, they didn't have their bundles with them."

"Well," laughed Mrs. Evans, "what's so unusual or suspicious about that?"

"Nothing, I suppose," replied Dolores, "but I happened to overhear part of what they were saying on the train. They were talking in Spanish and I understood just enough to gather that they are taking the same train that we are! They said something about a ship but I couldn't make out what it was. I'll bet they are mixed up in this business!"

"Nonsense!" smiled Mrs. Evans. "You're just letting your imagination run away with you. I suppose any one who takes the same train out to Long Island with us and talks about ships, is a suspicious character! Those men probably work in a ship yard some place on Long Island and were talking shop. Hurry up, now, pick out a pair of binoculars, we're keeping the others waiting."

CHAPTER III

Boarding the train that was to carry them to the opposite end of Long Island, into the fashionable Southampton section, the girls, Mrs. Evans and Mr. Baldwin studiously avoided further discussion of the adventure upon which they were embarked. Taking their cue from Mr. Baldwin who began to dwell at length on the advantages of a residence in Long Island, the girls and Mrs. Evans plied him with questions such as any prospective tenant might ask a renting agent. Matters such as water, gas, light, heat and electricity were earnestly discussed. Even Dolores forgot her suspicions concerning the two men she had seen and entered whole heartedly into the spirit of the moment. Mrs. Evans, however, noticed that each time the train stopped at a station, Dolores scrutinized each passenger as he entered or left the train. At length Mr. Baldwin announced that the next stop would be theirs and some minutes later when the train came to a halt and the little party assembled on the platform, the girls and Mrs. Evans were delighted with the scenic beauties before them.

The warm spring sun and gentle rains were turning the landscape into a fairyland of flowers and rioting colors while the strong salt breezes blowing in from the Sound gave the air an invigorating tang and freshness that caused the girls to draw in great, refreshing breaths. A dilapidated relic of the days when autos were a novelty stood at one end of the station and as Mr. Baldwin led the girls and Mrs. Evans in its direction, they saw two wide expanses of shoe leather protrude from the space formerly occupied by the windshield. Upon closer inspection the shoe leather was seen to be attached to two ebony sticks around which were draped what once had been the trousers of a person in the United States Naval service. A coat that had once glittered resplendently with gold braid, some of which was still in evidence, completed the rest of the ensemble, the entire affair encasing the sleeping frame of the one to whom the operation of the aged vehicle was entrusted. Standing on the running board, Mr. Baldwin reached over and, by dint of much rough shaking, woke the chauffeur of the only means of transportation in sight.

"Taxi, suh?" mumbled the sleeper drowsily, "Taxi? Any place in Sou'famptin fo' a haffa dolluh. Ga'ntees t' git yo' dar an' bring yo' back fo' fo' bits, suh."

"That's fine," laughed Mr. Baldwin. "I want you to take my clients and myself out to the old Dutton place. Do you know where it is and how to get there?"

At the mention of the name, the Negro's eyes opened wide and he looked at Mr. Baldwin in amazement. An idea seemed to be forming slowly in his brain.

"Did yo' all say de ol' Dutton place, suh?" he asked unbelievingly.

"That's the one," replied Mr. Baldwin. "Do you think this old bus can take us that far? I'll pay you double if you can make it without a breakdown."

"Oh, Ah guess us kin make it all right," assured the darky, "but is yo' all suah yo' wants de Dutton place? Don' yo' all mean some place else like de—like de—"

"No," interrupted Mr. Baldwin, "I said the Dutton place and I mean the Dutton place. What's the matter with it? Why don't you want us to go there?"

"Why golly, suh, don' yo' all know?" asked the Negro incredulously. "Dat place am haunted, sho' 'nuf. Dere ain' bin nobuddy eroun' dat dere ol' Dutton place fo' yeahs an' yeahs 'ceptin' dat crazy, no 'count Sam Hawkins an' his missus whut lives dere an' *dey* don' live in de big house. Naw sir! Dey lives in de li'l lodge down by de main gate. Dey ain' *no*-buddy whut goes t' de big house no mo'."

"Well, we're going there," replied Mr. Baldwin firmly, "and if you won't take us, I'll find somebody who will. Come on, girls, we can't stay here all day."

But as Mr. Baldwin, Mrs. Evans and the girls prepared to move off, the darky, loath to lose the opportunity, evidently all too rare in his life, of earning a few cents called them back and offered to drive them wherever they wished to go.

"Ah'll take yo' all up dar," he announced, "but Ah ain' gwine inter dat house."

"You don't have to go into the house," smiled Mr.

Baldwin, helping the girls and Mrs. Evans into the creaking old wreck. "Just take us there and wait for us."

As the machine bounced and jolted along, the girls and Mrs. Evans laughed at the darky's fears. Questioning brought forth the information that mysterious lights and noises had been emanating from the old mansion which investigation on the part of the local authorities showed to be nothing more than Mr. and Mrs. Hawkins, the caretakers, making the rounds of the deserted rooms with a lantern while the noises were blamed on the several dogs kept by the pair. This explanation had satisfied all but the picturesquely clad chauffeur and his people who firmly believed that the house was haunted. As time wore on, the rest of the population on that part of the island gradually accepted the Negroes' theory for no other reason than a topic of conversation and the old Dutton place became known as a haunted house.

Situated high on a hill on its own grounds, overlooking Long Island Sound, the house reared its weather beaten head above a tangle of tall trees and vines, its broad, sloping roof gleaming in the afternoon sun.

Cornelius Dutton had built the house a generation ago soon after he had amassed a fortune and, until some six or seven years ago, the family had occupied it, son following father. Then came financial reverses. Sydney Dutton, Cornelius' dissolute grandson, sold the house without authority or permission and absconded with the money. His father, Roger Dutton, unaware of his son's action, also sold the house and in the resultant legal entanglements, the property reverted to the government pending the outcome of the long drawn out court battles. Since the house was completely furnished, representing an investment of many hundreds of thousands of dollars, a caretaker and his wife were engaged to guard the property from invaders but simple Sam Hawkins felt too ill at ease living amidst the splendor of a by-gone day and moved into the gate keeper's lodge at the entrance to the large estate.

In the years that followed, the once well kept grounds became overgrown with a tangle of weeds and shrubbery and the attacks of wind and rain and lack of care began to manifest themselves in places around the massive house. The rooms and furniture, however, were a silent tribute to Sarah Hawkins' abilities as a housekeeper. Each morning she carried her mops, pails and dust cloths to the big house and while her husband patched up the more glaring ravages of time, she thoroughly cleaned one enormous room at a time. At night the mansion was plunged in darkness and only the booming of the surf, borne by the wind from the Sound, echoed through the silent rooms.

Occasionally, Sam would light a lantern, at his wife's request, and go through the deserted house, making sure all windows and doors were securely fastened. Returning from one such trip recently, Sam stopped at the little tool shed behind the comfortable, stone lodge he shared with his wife and as he entered the long, low living room, Sarah Hawkins looked up inquiringly at the tool box her husband brought with him. Lighting his pipe, Sam explained,

"I'm going to make a few traps," he announced. "I heard some scratching in the walls up there tonight. Rats or mice must have gotten in there somehow recently."

"Oh my gracious!" exclaimed his wife anxiously, "I hope they don't ruin all that lovely furniture! Couldn't we keep one of the dogs in there at night to scare them away? I wouldn't mind so much if I hadn't been so careful in cleaning up there."

"Don't you worry about it," her husband soothed, "I'll soon haul 'em out of there."

But despite Sam's efforts, the scratching continued and his most cleverly designed traps remained empty.

Bumping along the road from the railroad station to the old Dutton mansion, the ancient hack containing Mrs. Evans, Mabel, Dolores, Anita, Lenore, Alice and Mr. Baldwin wheezed and rattled under the unusual pressure put upon it by its dusky driver, anxious to earn the extra bonus promised by Mr. Baldwin.

Rounding a curve in the road, the aged vehicle suddenly jerked violently, uttered a despairing cough and with a final rattle of loose machinery, came to a standstill.

"Dar she is," pointed the darky, indicating a huge, wrought iron gate set in a stone wall along the opposite side of the road. "Dat's de gate. Ring de bell an' ef Sam Hawkins er his missus is eroun', dey'll let yo' all in but Ah dunno whut yo' all wants ter go messin' eroun' dere fo'. Dey ain' no good gwine ter come of sech things nohow, no *suh!* An' now, suh, effen yo'll kine'ly pay me mah fo' bits, Ah'll skedaddle back ter town. Ah got impo'tant business ter 'tend to, yassuh."

"You'll wait right here until I come back," laughed Mr. Baldwin as Mrs. Evans and the girls alighted from the car. "We're not going to walk all the way back."

From the road, all the girls and Mrs. Evans could see of the mansion were the tips of a chimney and a corner of the roof while barely discernible through the iron gate, parts of the gate keeper's lodge could be seen through the dense growth of trees and shrubs. A small push button was set into the stone work near the gate and as Mr. Baldwin placed his finger against it, several dogs of all sizes and breeds came rushing and barking furiously, intent on frightening the intruders away. A moment later, Sam Hawkins, tall and erect despite his advanced years, appeared through the trees and, after silencing the dogs, inquired, politely, of Mr. Baldwin, the reason for his visit, since strangers were a rarity at that place.

"Baldwin is my name," the government man began glibly, "I'm from the Homeland Real Estate company and I've come to show these ladies the property. They've expressed their interest in a place similar to this and if you don't mind, I'd like to show them around, just to give them an idea what a Long Island estate looks like."

"I don't mind," replied Hawkins, "but nobody told me this place was for sale or rent. I'm the caretaker here and I guess I ought to know. I'll let you in and you can look around all you want but I can't let you rent or sell the place. I don't even know who owns it and I guess nobody else does either. The government has charge of it now," he concluded, unlocking the heavy iron gate. "You'll have to ask them."

Unknown to them, however, the government had engaged Mr. and Mrs. Hawkins through a private individual, having first carefully investigated their records and found them satisfactory. Mr. Baldwin was therefore prepared to easily overcome whatever objections Hawkins might have to allowing the five Camp Fire girls and their leader to establish their residence, for the time being, on the Dutton estate. As Hawkins was about to lead the little party up the almost obscured gravel walk to the mansion, Mr. Baldwin tapped him on the shoulder and beckoned him into the lodge.

Puzzled, Hawkins followed, but a moment later, when both men re-appeared, Hawkins was wearing a broad smile and Mr. Baldwin was restoring some papers to his pocket. The girls and Mrs. Evans were delighted with the old house and as Mrs. Hawkins took them from room to room, their pleased expressions caused that honest soul to beam with joy. The house was lavishly furnished in the style prevalent when it was built but although long since outmoded, the furniture and decorations were still in an excellent state of preservation, thanks both to the superior quality of the appointments and Mrs. Hawkins' loving care. The large, high ceilinged rooms with their massive, carved oak fire places and long, latticed windows covered by heavy, velvet drapes, fascinated the admiring girls. Huge oil paintings set in massive, gilt frames hung against the mahogany paneled walls. Deep, rich carpeting covered some of the floors while others were left bare, revealing the highly polished parquetry of a day long since gone. In the library of the mansion, the walls were lined from ceiling to floor with row upon row of books. Placed about the room were deep, comfortable chairs, occasional tables and reading lamps. The bedrooms were almost as large as the rooms downstairs and as Mrs. Hawkins opened the doors to them, she told the thrilled girls and Mrs. Evans that linens for the ponderous, canopied beds, as well as mattresses were in storage in an especially constructed storeroom in another part of the house but she promised that the rooms would be ready for occupancy by nightfall. The plumbing system had been kept in repair by Sam Hawkins since, in her constant campaign against dirt in the big house, Sarah Hawkins required pail after pail of hot water that could not be otherwise obtained. In order to facilitate matters, it was agreed that Mr. and Mrs. Hawkins should move back into the mansion with Mrs. Evans and the girls, since in her role as cook, Sarah Hawkins would spend most of her time there while her husband would find plenty to do in the way of repairs. Returning from their tour of inspection, the girls and Mrs. Evans admitted they were genuinely in love with the old house and while Mr. Baldwin made financial arrangements with Sam Hawkins, the girls begged the protesting Mrs. Hawkins to allow them to help with the final preparations in making the house ready for their occupancy. Mr. Baldwin, however, settled the matter.

"Mr. and Mrs. Hawkins will take care of everything here," he told them. "You'd better come with me. I've got to arrange about having the electricity turned on here and installing telephone service and while I'm doing that, you girls can shop around for the dishes and kitchen utensils you'll need and anything else you think you ought to have. And that reminds me, you'll need a car to go to town in once in a while. I'll have one sent down from the city," he concluded as the little group left the house, "and in case you need any money, I'll open an account for you at the bank here. Now let's see if our trusty chariot is still waiting for us."

As the girls, Mrs. Evans and Mr. Baldwin reached the entrance gate, they saw the ancient automobile parked across the road where they had left it but its dark skinned driver was nowhere in sight. Approaching the car, they looked inside it and all around but the chauffeur evidently had wandered off, or so they thought until Mr. Baldwin, reaching up, squeezed the rubber bulb that blew the horn. As the hoarse grunts emitted by that aged arrangement echoed across the fields, a sound, muffled and sleepy came from beneath the car, followed by the tattered form of the driver. Rising slowly to his feet, he carefully brushed the dirt from his rags and looked reproachfully at Mr. Baldwin, shaking his head from side to side.

"Don' evah do dat agin'," he warned, "yo' all like ter have blowed mah brains out! Dat hawn stick down right close ter mah haid an' Ah wuz sleepin' so nice, too."

"But," laughed Mrs. Evans as she and the girls climbed into the car, "aren't these seats softer to sleep on than the hard road? I'm sure they're cleaner."

"Yas'm," agreed the Negro, "them seats is cleanuh an' softuh but y' see, ma'm, dey ain' got no shade to 'em nohow an' dis sun gits pow'ful hot long erbout dis time ob de yeah. Yo' all ain' fixin' ter live in dat ol' Dutton place, is yo'?"

"They are," replied Mr. Baldwin, "and until their car arrives from the city, you are going to be their chauffeur and if they like you well enough, you'll stay on."

"Ah—Ah's a pow'ful bad actuh, suh," protested the Negro in alarm, "an' besides Ah got impo'tant business ter 'tend to. Ah ain' gwine ter live in no hanted house!"

A bill pressed into a dusky palm silenced all protests and a short while later the relic wheezed into the little Long Island town and while Mr. Baldwin went about his various duties, Mrs. Evans and the girls began their shopping tour. Going from one store to another, Dolores suddenly clutched Mrs. Evans' arm.

"There they are!" she whispered in alarm, "walking on the other side of the street!"

"Who?" asked the Camp Fire leader in surprise, looking about her.

"Those two men I told you about, the ones we saw in the subway train. They're here!"

CHAPTER IV

Following the direction of Dolores' gaze, Mrs. Evans saw the backs of two men as they walked down the opposite side of the street. One was slightly taller than the other and both were gesticulating wildly with their hands and jabbering excitedly. At the corner, they parted and as they disappeared from sight, Mrs. Evans turned to Dolores while the other girls, who had walked on ahead, returned to see what had attracted the attention of their leader and Dolores. Mrs. Evans smiled.

"Dolores has you beaten as investigators," she told the others. "She has two suspicious persons on her list already. She found them in the subway to-day."

"Who are they?" asked Anita, wide eyed, "where are they? What do they look like?"

"Why didn't you tell us before?" demanded Mabel. "Are they here some place?"

But when Dolores told the others what she had seen and heard, Lenore threw back her head and burst into laughter while Alice giggled at her friend's alarm.

"I saw them too," laughed Lenore, "and had the same idea you had, especially since they were talking in a foreign language. I told Alice to tell you to listen to what they were saying because it sounded like Spanish and I know you understand it. Tell her what you saw, Alice," Lenore chuckled, turning to the blonde Camp Fire girl.

"Didn't you see those little tickets in their hats?" giggled Alice merrily. "Your suspicious characters are a couple of subway track walkers. Those tickets said so."

"But what are they doing out here?" asked Dolores, puzzled. "There aren't any subways here and they certainly don't live here. I still think there's something queer about them. And then, what happened to the bundles they were carrying? I'm going to keep an eye on those two fellows if I ever see them again."

Their shopping tour completed, Mrs. Evans and the girls returned to the broken down old car and its somnolent driver to await Mr. Baldwin's return. Dolores had announced her intention of acquainting the government man with the facts about the two men and when he returned, he listened carefully while she repeated what she had told Mrs. Evans and the others. When she had finished, Mr. Baldwin smiled.

"I'm sorry to disappoint you," he smiled, "but they probably do live here. There's a section near here inhabited by working people of that class. However, it wouldn't hurt matters any to keep an eye on them but don't give them all your attention to the exclusion of everything else. Your chief job, you know, is to watch the Sound for any suspicious looking craft and to investigate anything out of the ordinary going on."

Sitting in the dilapidated car while its driver dozed peacefully against the steering wheel, Mr. Baldwin gave the five Camp Fire girls and their young leader final instructions, since he was returning to New York City on the next train.

"Don't go snooping around like a pack of hungry wolves," he told them. "Just act as though you were at home. When the weather gets warmer, you can go swimming in the Sound or take hikes through the woods around here or do whatever you please. But wherever you go or whatever you do, be constantly on the alert and above all, watch the Sound for suspicious looking boats. Those smugglers are operating some place in this vicinity and it's up to you to investigate those operations."

After Mr. Baldwin's departure, Mrs. Evans woke the sleeping chauffeur and the six Federal Investigators returned to the scene of their duties. As they rattled and bumped along, Mabel, who was sitting in the back seat with Lenore, Dolores and Mrs. Evans, leaned over and tapped the driver on the shoulder. Anita and Alice were sitting on the front seat next to the darky and thinking that one of them had tapped his shoulder as a signal for him to move over and thus give them more room, he twisted his body sideways. The result brought screams of alarm from the other occupants of the car for in turning about, the Negro twisted the steering wheel from its place atop the steering column of the car. With a wild lurch, the aged machine plunged across the road and, although there were no obstacles in its path, the aged wreck seemed to be looking for some object against which to end its unhappy existence. Despite the girls' screams of alarm, the dusky driver seemed entirely unperturbed. With a quick motion, he stopped the car, replaced the steering wheel and calmly proceeded on his way, as the others relaxed with relief.

"I didn't know you were so ticklish," Mabel exclaimed as they drove on. "I only wanted to ask you what your name is. We've got to call you something, you know."

"Oh, wuz dat you?" asked the darky in surprise, looking around. "Ah sho' thought one ob dese ladies up front heah tapped me t' move ovah so's dey cud have mo' room."

"Does this—er—car come apart so easily very often?" asked Alice timidly.

"Oh no'm," replied the darky earnestly, "dey's days when ha'dly nuthin flops off at all an' den ag'in dey's times when Ah has de ha'dest job keepin' 'er so'tuh in one piece. H'it jes' kinder depends on de weathuh, Ah guess. Ah dunno. Did you' all want ter know what mah name is?" he continued, turning around again to face Mabel and upon receiving a nod in reply from her, he cleared his throat nosily.

"Well, ma'm," he went on, "yo' has yo' choice. Some ob de folkses eroun' heah calls me de General on account ob mah unifawm an' othuhs jes' calls me plain Joe. But when mah Pappy git hisse'f good an' mad, he call me by mah right name, he sho' do."

"And what is your right name?" asked Mrs. Evans as the car stopped by the iron gate.

"Mah right name," announced the Negro proudly, alighting to help the girls and Mrs. Evans from the car, "is Josephus Abraham Lincoln Geo'ge Washin'ton Petuh Simms."

"That's enough to make anybody mad," giggled Lenore as the little party crossed the road. "Suppose we just call you Joe and let it go at that? It'll be easier."

"Suits me," agreed Joe. "Now whut yo' all want me ter do fo' yo' all today?"

"Why, there's nothing I can think of right now," smiled Mrs. Evans as Sam Hawkins arrived to open the gate for them. "But where can I reach you in case we do want you? Do you live very far away from here? Could you come back tomorrow morning?"

"Ah could do dat," Joe replied. "Ah lives ovah at de udder end ob town but Ah kin drive ovah heah mawnin's. Ef yo' wants me any udder time ob de day, yo' all jes' phone de railroad station er de Oceanside Drug sto' an' ax fo' de General, dat's me."

"Wait a minute!" cried Anita suddenly as Joe turned to go. "What about our luggage?"

"That's right," answered Mrs. Evans, "I'd almost forgotten about that. I'll give Joe a note to the baggage master at the station to turn our bags over to him and he can bring them out here as soon as they arrive. You won't forget, will you, Joe?"

Assuring the Camp Fire leader that the luggage would be in her possession as soon as possible after the train bearing it arrived, Joe took the note Mrs. Evans gave him and returned to the little Long Island town. Following the caretaker back through the trees to the mansion the six Federal Investigators were to call home, they were surprised to see the progress Sarah Hawkins had made during their absence. Snowy white linen covered the beds and the boards had been removed from most of the windows. The many purchases they had made in town had arrived shortly before their return and while Mrs. Hawkins busied herself in the spacious kitchen preparing the evening meal, the girls and Mrs. Evans set off on a tour of exploration through the old house. Opening a door leading from the enormous living room, the girls stepped into a room that was plunged in darkness. About to withdraw for fear of knocking over and breaking some valuable ornament unseen in the gloom, the girls jumped in surprise as the room suddenly became flooded with brilliant light and they saw that they were standing on the threshold of a large ball room while at the other end, his hand on the electric switch, stood Sam Hawkins, smiling broadly at them.

"The man from the illuminating company was just here," he explained, coming toward them, "and turned on the electricity. I was just going around seeing that all the lights were working properly. It

certainly seems good to have light in the old house
a ain. Do you think you're going to like your new
l me? I hope you won't feel crowded," he laughed.
"There are only thirty-six rooms here, you know,
told."

"Golly!" ex imed Mabel. "Thirty-six rooms!
e could sta a hotel with less!"

Contin g their tour of the house, aided now
b a w n of illumination, the girls and Mrs. Evans
r ac the third floor of the mansion. A door near
th ead of the stairs opened into a large, airy, well
li hted room that, from its furnishings and wall
paper, they knew had once been a nursery. A huge
dormer window occupying almost all of one wall
afforded a clear, uninterrupted view of Long Island
and a long, wide strip of white sand that was
the beach. A small pier projected out into the water
while next to it stood a squat, windowless building,
erected on piles near the water's edge. Daylight was
rapidly fading and as the girls and Mrs. Evans
gazed out at the majestic scene before them, white-caps began to form on the crests of the inrushing
waves, gleaming like phosphorus in the semi-gloom.
Far in the distance the outlines of a lighthouse was
barely discernible while directly below them and as
far almost as the beach, tangled tree tops and inter-lacing vines and branches met the gaze of the thrilled
girls and their leader. Suddenly Alice sighed.

"The rest of you can have the downstairs bed-rooms," she murmured dreamily, "but I want this room for my own. I'll fix it up to look like a ship's cabin and——"

"Get seasick," snickered Mabel. "Just listen to that surf booming out there. I don't see how you'd be able to sleep with that racket going on all night. I admit the view is beautiful but that continuous noise would drive me crazy in no time."

"You wouldn't have far to go," laughed Lenore. "But I think Alice has a good idea. One of us should be up here at all times to keep a lookout for those suspicious looking boats Mr. Baldwin told us to watch for. Alice could do it at night while the rest of us took turns at it during the day. I'm even willing to share this room with her. If anything happens out there during the night, one of us will hear it."

And although she was loath to share the room with anyone, Alice was forced to agree to Lenore's suggestion, since, as Mr. Baldwin had told them, a large part of their investigations concerned keeping a sharp lookout on the Sound.

The succeeding days the girls and Mrs. Evans spent in exploring the grounds of the old estate, forcing their way through underbrush and trees to find remains of once beautiful gardens, broad terraces and crumbling statuary. A border of broken and moss grown blue tile set in a small declevity not far from the house told the girls that once there had been a swimming pool there. Anita, however, was puzzled and said so.

"Why," she reasoned, "should they want a swimming pool with the whole ocean and Long Island

Sound practically at their front door? It seems superfluous, doesn't it?"

"It might, to you or me," agreed Alice who was standing nearby, "but these people had the money to gratify their slightest whim. The Sound might have been too cold or too rough or too far away for whoever built this pool. And then again," she suddenly exclaimed, "it might not have been a swimming pool at all! Let's see!"

Dropping to her hands and knees while the bewildered Anita looked on, Alice began digging the earth with her fingers around one of the tiles that formed a square around some bushes. The ground, softened by the spring rains, yielded easily to the Camp Fire girl's exploring fingers and a moment later, with a triumphant cry she extracted the tile from its resting place and pointed to where it had been.

"Look, Anita!" she exclaimed excitedly, "What do you see? My guess was correct!"

Squatting down next to her friend, Anita looked at the soft, black earth and poked an exploring finger into it and then looked perplexedly at Alice for an explanation.

"All I see is dirt," she replied. "What else is there to see? Elves or something?"

"This is not, nor ever was, a swimming pool," explained Alice, her voice trembling with excitement. "These tiles were placed around here to mark a location! If this had been a swimming pool, there would have been a cement foundation under this tile!"

"By jingo that's right!" cried Anita. "What do you suppose this space was marked off for? I'll bet there's something buried under here! I wonder what it is?"

"We'll soon find out," promised Alice, rising. "Come on, we'll get the others and start digging. I wonder if Mr. Hawkins has any shovels and pick axes on the place?"

Pushing their way back through the dense undergrowth, Alice and Anita soon came upon Dolores, Mabel, Lenore and Mrs. Evans, gathered around a huge marble urn that had been toppled from its pedestal and was lying in several pieces on the ground. As the two girls approached, Lenore looked up and beckoned them to join her and the others.

"You're just in time," she announced, "to help us carry this beautiful thing back to the house. We're going to try to put it back together again."

"You only think you are," replied Anita. "We've got something more important for you to do. Tell these pot pasters what you discovered, Alice," she concluded and as Alice told the others about her theory of the blue tiles, the marble urn was forgotten in the thrill of the new discovery. Eager to find out if anything were really buried within the blue border, the girls were about to set off for the caretaker's lodge in quest of picks and shovels when the deep, metallic boom of a brass gong reached their ears. A quick glance at her watch told Mrs. Evans her ears had not deceived her. So engrossed had she and the girls been in exploring the old estate that all sense of time had been completely forgotten in the excitement.

"My gracious!" she exclaimed, "it's six o'clock already! I'm afraid we'll have to let the digging go until tomorrow. That was Mrs. Hawkins calling us in to supper."

As the six Federal Investigators trooped back to the house, they exchanged ideas concerning what might, if anything, be buried in the small declevity marked off by the border of blue tiles. Mabel suggested buried treasure but Dolores suddenly snapped her fingers as a more plausible idea occurred to her. Swiftly she told the others of the theory that had just entered her mind and as the six went upstairs to wash and change clothes before dining, it was agreed to return to the scene of Alice's discovery that night, provided Sam Hawkins could supply digging tools.

"Did it ever occur to you," Dolores had suddenly exclaimed, "that those smugglers might have their contraband goods hidden there and marked the place with those tiles for other members of their outfit to find? The Sound isn't far from here. They could easily land their cargo on the beach and carry it up here to hide until they were ready to get rid of it when they'd dig it up and take it away!" The girls and Mrs. Evans were complimenting Dolores on her solution of the mystery when a sudden muffled exclamation from Lenore as she slipped her dress on over her head caused them to turn around. Wiggling through the garment, she shook her head.

"I'm sorry, Dolores," she said, "but I just happened to think of one flaw in your theory that makes the whole thing impossible. There's a high stone wall all around this place and we're on a main road. Even if the smugglers did manage, somehow, to get their heavy cargo over the wall, somebody would have seen them long before now and reported the activity to the authorities and if that were the case, we wouldn't be here now. Maybe those tiles were just put there to mark off a flower bed or a statue or a fountain. I don't think there'd be any use in digging there anyhow, at least, not tonight. I think we can safely wait until tomorrow sometime, don't you?"

Forced to admit the logic of Lenore's reasoning, Dolores reluctantly gave up the idea of returning to the blue tile border that night.

CHAPTER V

Although Alice and Lenore slept in the large room on the third floor, they kept most of their clothes in one of the many unoccupied bedrooms on the second floor merely to be with the others in case, as Alice explained it, both should need some assistance with their toilettes at the same time.

As the girls and Mrs. Evans, their preparations finished, left their rooms, Alice, instead of following them downstairs turned and began mounting the steps leading to the third floor. Noticing her action Mrs. Evans called after her, telling her she would keep the others waiting for supper. But Alice continued up the stairs, taking two at a time in her haste and calling over her shoulder to Mrs. Evans and the rest of the girls below her not to wait.

"I'll only be a minute," she announced as she reached the top landing. "Go ahead."

Reaching her room, Alice swiftly pulled open a bureau drawer and taking the pair of powerful marine binoculars Mr. Baldwin had purchased, turned her attention to the larger dormer window and the tossing waves of Long Island Sound outside. For a full minute she scanned the water but all that came into her line of vision was the lighthouse, standing grim and lonely far away. So powerful were the glasses, however, that Alice was able to make out the tiny figure of a man standing on the small balcony that encircled the top of the lighthouse. Fascinated, she watched the microscopic figure move about until it disappeared from view inside the lighthouse and then, returning the binoculars to the bureau drawer, she left the room to join the others downstairs.

After supper, plans were made to return to the blue tiles early the next morning and begin excavations. In response to their inquiries, Sam Hawkins promised each girl a pick and shovel but before he left the big house for the night, he imparted a word of advice that Mrs. Evans smilingly agreed to take.

"The brush around here is pretty thick," he informed the Camp Fire leader. "Better phone and have Joe come up in the morning so he and I can clear most of it away for you. We'll help you with the digging, too, if you want us to and from what I know about digging," he finished with a laugh, "I think you'll want us to. That's a pretty large plot of ground up there and it's going to take a lot of work to turn it all over. Well, I hope you find what you're looking for tomorrow. Goodnight."

After Hawkins left, Mabel seated herself at the beautifully polished Grand piano in a far corner of the big room and although the instrument was woefully out of tune, she managed to play fairly accurate interpretations of various popular songs as well as the lovely Camp Fire melodies while the others gathered around her and sang. Wearying at length of playing, Mabel rose from the piano and while Alice took her place, she wandered over to one of the large windows and thrusting aside the heavy red velvet drapes, looked out at the moonlit scene below her. From where she stood, Mabel could see down the tree covered side of the hill on which the house was built to where a portion of the stone wall surrounding the estate formed a parallel line with the road just before it curved away toward the Sound. Beyond the road, Mabel could catch a glimpse of white sand gleaming in the moonlight and an occasional reflection of the moonbeams as they danced across the water. Opening the latch, Mabel swung the two sections of the tall window wide open and as the soft warm spring breezes wafted across the room, bringing with them the tang of salt air, she turned impulsively to the others, interrupting the song they were singing.

"It's too nice out tonight to stay in the house," she announced. "Let's go down to the beach. And incidentally, that reminds me, we didn't bring our bathing suits along."

As the others greeted Mabel's suggestion with enthusiasm, Mrs. Evans smiled to herself and, excusing herself for a moment, slipped upstairs, re-appearing a second later with a package under her arm. In answer to the girls' questions, she merely opened the bundle, revealing six brightly colored bathing suits.

"You think of everything," laughed Lenore holding a bright yellow suit against herself to see if it were the correct size. "May we initiate them to-night, please?"

But despite the girls' pleadings, Mrs. Evans remained firm in her refusal to allow them to go swimming, explaining that the weather was not yet warm enough nor were they sufficiently acquainted with the surf to venture into it for the first time at night. Restoring the suits to the box she had taken them from, Mrs. Evans left the package lying on a table and soon she and the girls were on their way down to the beach, situated across the road from the big house. Guided by the light from the caretaker's lodge, the little group soon reached the main gate which Sam Hawkins promised to leave unlocked until their return. The fine, warm evening had brought many automobiles out on the road going past the estate and as the girls and Mrs. Evans stood by the roadside, waiting for an opportunity to cross, Anita turned to Mrs. Evans.

"I thought Mr. Baldwin said he was going to send us a car from the city," she said. "We've been here a few days already. Do you think he forgot about it or us?"

"I don't think he's forgotten," replied Mrs. Evans. "He's probably a very busy man and just hasn't had time to get around to it. But why do you ask? Is there something you need a car for? Joe could drive you wherever you wanted to go, you know."

"Oh, I don't want to go any place," replied Anita. "Seeing all these machines just reminded me of it. I wish they'd stop a minute so we could get across the road."

A few seconds later, the traffic decreased sufficiently to allow the girls and Mrs. Evans to scurry across. Walking along the narrow strip of grass at the roadside, they soon came to a flight of weed grown stone stairs leading down to the beach. Following cautiously where they led, testing each step before treading on it, the girls and Mrs. Evans finally reached the gleaming white strip of sand. A bright moon and a clear night provided perfect and distinct visibility and as the six Federal Investigators strolled along the beach they had no difficulty in seeing and identifying the various shapes that formed a sharp silhouette against the night sky. The squat, windowless building next to the old pier at the water's edge that the girls had seen from the nursery window was a boathouse, they saw as they reached and inspected it. The wide, double doors of the shack faced and projected over the water so the girls were unable to look in but as Mrs. Evans leaned against the side of the building for support while she poured the sand from her shoes, she suddenly bent closer, listening intently while she waved her dainty satin pump in the air for silence. Immediately the others in swift silence crowded close, pressing their ears against the rough boards of the boathouse. For a second or two they heard nothing, then suddenly a scraping sound reached their ears, following by a series of slowly spaced bumps and again silence.

"There's a boat in there!" whispered Mrs. Evans, replacing her shoe. "A motor boat!"

"How do you know it's a motor boat?" asked Dolores. "Can you see anything there?"

"You don't have to see anything," Alice answered for Mrs. Evans. "Can't you smell the gasoline and oil? I wonder whose boat it is? I don't think it's Mr. Hawkins'."

"Why not?" asked Lenore. "It's perfectly logical that he should own a motor boat."

"Well, if this is his boat," replied Anita, "why didn't he tell us about it before?"

"Oh, he probably forgot," explained Mabel, "and besides, we never asked him about one."

"Just the same," announced Alice sitting down on the sand, "I'm going to try and get a look at it if for nothing else than future identification, and mere curiosity." As Alice began pulling off her shoes and stockings, the other girls, with cries of delight, dropped down on the sand and began following suit, Mrs. Evans joining them. Carefully rolling up their skirts, the five Camp Fire girls and their leader thrust bare wriggling toes tentatively into the water and finding it surprisingly warm, stepped boldly in and began wading out to the front of the boathouse. The tide was out and so even Alice, who was the smallest of the group, experienced no difficulty in keeping her clothes dry. Turning a corner of the building, Mabel, who was the first to arrive in front of the boathouse, uttered a cry of despair and as the others joined her, she pointed to a glittering object fastened to the boathouse doors high above their heads. Reflecting the moon's bright beams, a heavy lock held both doors securely closed against their invasion. For a moment the six Federal Investigators stood where they were in the waters of Long Island Sound. Then suddenly Lenore bent down, close to the doors and thrust her hand into the water. Straightening up a moment later, she announced an important discovery that brought new hope to the others.

"Look!" she pointed. "These doors don't quite reach to the water. We can easily swim under them and come up alongside the boat. We won't have to tamper with the lock either, so whoever owns the boat will never know we were here. Let's do it now!"

"I see you're determined to get your swim tonight," laughed Mrs. Evans, "but you're not going to do it with your clothes on. You'd catch cold by the time you got back to the house. The water is warmer than I thought it would be," she added, "let's go back for our bathing suits and then we'll find out what sort of boat this is here."

"If it's Mr. Hawkins' boat," Anita suggested as they waded back to shore, "we won't have to bother swimming under the boathouse. Let's ask him first before we change."

But Sam Hawkins knew of no boat in the squat building on the beach and in reply to the girls' questions could only advance the opinion that if there was a vessel of some sort in the boathouse, it had probably been left there by the last occupant of the

Dutton estate, in which case, it was ready to fall apart from neglect and rot.

"I've spent most of my life in sight of the Sound," Hawkins confessed, "but I don't believe I've been out in a boat more than twice in all that time, much less own one."

As Hawkins finished speaking, the girls and Mrs. Evans looked comprehendingly at one another. If the caretaker was not the owner of the boat, who was? The six Federal Investigators knew that a boat left continuously in the water for six or seven years would have sunk long before now and if their ears had not deceived them a while ago on the beach, the vessel in the boathouse was very much afloat! Keenly alert now and thrilled with expectancy, the girls and Mrs. Evans raced up the almost obliterated gravel path to the big house and too eager to take the time to run upstairs to change, since their bathing suits were already downstairs, they snatched them from the package Mrs. Evans had left lying on the table and donned the brightly colored garments where they were, in the spacious living room.

Stopping only to slip on their shoes since the gravel walk leading from the house and the stone steps going down to the beach would prove too severe on tender feet, the excited girls and Mrs. Evans raced from the house, halting for a moment at the lodge by the gate to ask Mrs. Hawkins to follow them with towels and robes.

As they stood by the side of the road, waiting an opportunity to cross, Sam Hawkins appeared at the massive iron gate, holding a shining object in his hand. Giving it to Mrs. Evans as Sarah Hawkins arrived with the towels and bathrobes, he pointed heavenward. The moon had slipped behind a cloud and instead of the silvery brightness of a few minutes ago, the surrounding landscape was plunged in black darkness.

"Here's a flashlight," he explained, "you might need it going down those steps."

"Oh, thank you," smiled Mrs. Evans and then turning to Mrs. Hawkins, she added, "it won't be necessary for you to come along, if you don't care to. We can carry our own towels and robes. I only thought we'd save time by asking you to bring them so we wouldn't have to wait but it seems as though this traffic knows we're in a hurry and is determined not to let us cross. We should dig a tunnel under the road."

Relinquishing the towels and robes, Mrs. Hawkins returned with her husband to the lodge and a moment later, the flow of traffic having momentarily ceased, the five Camp Fire girls and their leader ran across the road. Lighting their way with the flashlight down the stone steps, they reached the beach and as they approached the boathouse, its bright beams revealed something that had escaped their notice during their first visit. At the back of the windowless shack and facing the beach, was a small door, secured, unlike the large double doors in front, with a strong patent lock. A glance at the lock further disproved Sam Hawkins' theory that the boathouse had been unused since its last owner's departure, for far from being old and rusty, it shone with newness. Kicking off their shoes, the girls and Mrs. Evans waded out to the front of the boathouse. Handing the flashlight to Dolores, Mrs. Evans dove under the water, coming to the surface a moment later in the darkness of the boathouse. Bending down, she called to the others to follow her.

"Hand me the flashlight first," she called, "and be careful not to get it wet, then the rest of you come in here. The water is shallow, so don't dive deep and be careful not to bang your heads on the doors."

Swiftly and in rapid succession, the five Camp Fire girls dove and swam under the big double doors of the boathouse to join their leader. As they bobbed up on the other side, they looked about them in amazement for all the searching beams of the flashlight in Mrs. Evans' hand revealed were four rough wooden walls and a small landing platform in front of the back door! As the girls stood waist deep in the chilly waters of the dank interior, they were too surprised and disappointed to know what to say. They had been positive the sounds they heard before were made by a boat thumping against the side of the building and even now, the strong smell of gasoline and oil assailed their nostrils but the boat supposedly responsible for all three circumstances was strangely missing! As Mrs. Evans cast the bright beams of her light on the water, Lenore suddenly pointed to her waist where a band of rainbow hued, viscid oil clung, completely encircling the young Camp Fire leader.

"There was a boat in here!" she cried. "Look at that oil! Somebody came and took it away while we were gone! I wonder if they knew we had been here and skipped?"

"There was a motor boat of some kind in here all right," agreed Mabel, "but why didn't we hear it leave? The night is quiet and those things make an awful racket. We should have heard it long ago, anyway. A fine bunch of investigators, we are—not!"

"Maybe we didn't hear it because of the booming of the surf," suggested Anita.

"Well, the surf isn't booming tonight," replied Dolores, "and we still didn't hear it. The house is probably too far away for the sound to carry that distance."

"I don't care what happened to the boat," shivered Alice, her teeth chattering, "it's cold in here. I'm going back to the house. The rest of you can stay here if you want to and freeze. Brrrr! This would be a good place to come to sometime in August."

Standing in front of the little landing platform, Alice had been swinging her arms around in an effort to keep warm and as she finished speaking, she struck her elbow against the edge of the landing. Jumping away in pain and rubbing the bruised arm tenderly, she cast a malevolent glance at the platform while Mrs. Evans directed the rays of the flashlight toward her. As the beams fell on the rough wooden planking Alice forgot her pain and seizing the flashlight from Mrs. Evans, churned the water to a foam in her haste to reach the little platform while the others looked on in bewilderment. Needing both hands for what she was about to do, Alice handed the torch to Lenore, directing her to play its beams along the edge of the landing and then gripping the protruding plank, pushed upward with all her strength. Seeing what she was trying to accomplish, the others came to her aid and under their combined efforts, the floor of the landing platform slowly raised up, like the lid of a box!

CHAPTER VI

Reaching up, Lenore thrust her flashlight into the opening thus revealed. Peering over the edge of the platform that Alice's action had suddenly converted into a box, Mrs. Evans and the girls saw a short flight of rough, wooden steps leading downward, followed by a narrow strip of planking that evidently formed part of a floor.

"A storage room!" gasped Mabel, following the direction of the flashlight's beams.

"It's more than that," supplemented Alice, boosting herself out of the water and on to the edge of the platform. "It looks as though this might be the beginning of a tunnel! I'm going to find out. Who wants to come along? I'll bet a cookie we're on the trail of those smugglers, all right! This probably leads to their hideout!"

"But we can't go down there now!" protested Dolores. "It's chilly and drafty down there and all we have on is our bathing suits! And besides, we'd get our feet all full of splinters on these rough boards! Let's go back and get dressed first."

"And then how would we get back in here?" scoffed Anita. "I'm for going with Alice."

"So am I," added Lenore, "but wouldn't it be better to wait until daylight?"

"Silly!" laughed Mrs. Evans. "It would be just

as dark down there during the day as it is now. However, I think Dolores is right, we should be more warmly dressed than we are now. We could very easily slip some dry clothing under those doors without getting them wet, change in here and then explore this tunnel or whatever it is in comfort. And," she concluded, "I think we'd all better get back to the house now before we catch cold. It's chilly in here and this water isn't any too warm, either."

Lowering the platform, the girls and Mrs. Evans began wading toward the front of the boathouse to dive under the locked doors when the faint sound of rippling water reached their ears. Knowing her white arms would be visible in the darkness to the five girls behind her, Mrs. Evans spread them out and as the others seeing their leader's signal, halted, the rippling sound came nearer and louder, followed by the muffled tones of men's voices. Suddenly there was a sharp bump as some heavy object collided gently with the large double doors but Mrs. Evans waited to hear no more. Turning swiftly about, she whispered a terse command and six dim figures dropped silently into the water and swam back to the landing platform. As the girls raised the heavy lid, the rattle of the padlock against the steel hasp was heard and a moment later, the six Federal Investigators, climbing over the side of the platform, huddled in a group on the first of the flight of wooden stairs. As they swiftly but gently lowered the lid down over their heads, they saw the big double doors swing inward, revealing the dark outlines of a motor boat!

With a low, faintly audible sound from its engine, the boat glided into the shelter of the boathouse. Silently retreating further down the stairs, the girls and Mrs. Evans listened breathlessly while the men spoke. Suddenly Mabel grasped her leader's arm wildly.

"Suppose they come down here and find us?" she whispered. "We'd better turn around and see where this thing leads us now, before it's too late! Come on, they're getting out of the boat! They'll be coming down here any minute now. I can hear them!"

Even as Mabel spoke, the voices of the men became more audible and they heard the sound of their heavy footsteps on the platform as they stepped from the boat. Because of the scraping of their feet on the boards above them, the girls were unable to hear what the men were saying but rather than tarry at the risk of discovery, Mrs. Evans, acting on Mabel's suggestion, motioned to the excited girls to retreat. Moving slowly, lest a squeaking board give them away, their bare feet making no sound against the rough wooden planks, the six Federal Investigators backed away from the stairway until the sounds overhead were no longer heard. The searching rays of the flashlight showed them their surroundings. The same heavy planks that formed the floor of the tunnel also comprised its walls and ceiling with an occasional, rough archway built of wide, sturdy beams to lend support to the entire structure. The tunnel sloped upward, curving slightly to the left and as the girls, with Mrs. Evans, holding the flashlight, in the lead, followed its course, they wondered where it was leading them and what they would find at its end. The tunnel was wide enough to permit the girls to walk two abreast and as Anita and Lenore, who were following behind Mrs. Evans and Alice while Dolores and Mabel brought up the rear, looked about them, both Alice and Lenore uttered a surprised exclamation at the same time and both began talking simultaneously in their haste.

"The tunnel's getting wider!" announced Lenore, spreading her arms out to both walls. "When we started going through here, I could barely touch the walls and now I can't!"

"And look!" cried Alice, pointing to the floor, "wheel tracks! They must have been made by steel wheels to have dug so deeply into the wood. I wonder what caused them?"

"Wheels, probably," replied Mabel dryly, "or do you think they grew there recently?"

Stopping to examine the ruts worn into the wood flooring of the tunnel, Mrs. Evans agreed with Alice that they must have been made by steel or iron wheels since the edges of the ruts were torn and splintered as though by some hard, sharp instrument.

"Look," pointed Mrs. Evans, holding her flashlight close to the floor, "those wheels must have passed over here only recently. Some of these splinters are still new!"

Wondering what part wheels could have played

and evidently were still playing, in the tunnel, the girls and Mrs. Evans continued on their way. They had only proceeded a few feet, however, when Mrs. Evans suddenly stopped. The light from the electric torch Sam Hawkins had given her revealed a fairly wide space before them, large enough for the five Camp Fire girls and their leader to stand about in without crowding. Taking a few steps forward, Mrs. Evans saw that the tunnel, instead of continuing in a straight line, now branched off into two forks, one going to the right and the other to the left, the space in which the girls found themselves standing forming a sort of division between the portion of the tunnel they had just left and the two forks before them.

As Mrs. Evans sent the beams of her light around the walls and over the floor, Dolores suddenly sprang forward and dropped to her hands and knees, calling to Mrs. Evans to throw the light in her direction.

"See," she exclaimed excitedly as the rays of light fell on the floor near her, "the wheel tracks curve around here and go into this side of the tunnel! But there are no wheel tracks going into the other side! I wonder what that means, now?"

"That this is evidently the end of the main line," giggled Mabel, "and those other tracks are just a spur leading to a vacation resort back in the hills some place."

Paying no attention to Mabel, however, the others dropped to their hands and knees near Dolores and began examining the floor also. In the bright rays of the flashlight they had no difficulty in tracing the tracks along the floor to where they entered the left fork of the tunnel. Examination of the floor leading to and in front of the right fork, however, failed to reveal any tracks whatsoever and as the girls rose to their feet, they wondered which way to continue, right or left. The complete silence all about them assured them they were not being followed by the men who brought the boat to the windowless shack on the beach where the tunnel had its beginning and so now, relieved of the necessity of haste through fear, they calmly considered which course to pursue. Dolores, however, solved the problem with ease.

"There are six of us here," she began. "Three of us can follow one branch and the other three can follow the other. Both forks must lead some place. We can all meet later at the house and compare notes and if both these branches end up in a space similar to this, we can meet here and go back the way we came to the boathouse."

Her plan meeting instant approval, Dolores, taking Alice and Mabel, set off into the dark recesses of the left while Mrs. Evans, Lenore and Anita, went to the right.

Due to continuous use over a protracted period of time, the flashlight was fast losing its brilliance but rather than leave it behind as a tell-tale symbol of their presence in the tunnel, Mrs. Evans took it with her as she led Lenore and Alice into the darkness of the right branch of the tunnel. Feeling their way slowly and cautiously through the pitch blackness that surrounded them, the two Camp Fire girls and their leader walked in single file, hands on each other's shoulders. Although they were unable to penetrate the gloom with their eyes, the necessity of bending forward in order to maintain their balance told them they were walking uphill.

In the meantime, Dolores, Alice and Mabel, following the wheel tracks that disappeared into the left fork of the tunnel, also found it necessary to bend sharply from the waist in order to keep their equilibrium. The left fork of the tunnel in which they found themselves seemed to be wider than the other for, after a bit of careful maneuvering, the three girls found that it was possible for them to walk abreast.

Clasping hands, they moved slowly through the darkness that surrounded them, feeling cautiously with their bare feet for the rough, splintered ruts in the floor in order to avoid them. Since their progress was of necessity so slow, it seemed to the three Camp Fire girls that the tunnel would never end but would go on and on for ever.

"Maybe," whispered Alice as they crept along, "we've stumbled into an old subway. These ruts might have been where the original tracks were or were going to be."

"In that case," sighed Mabel, "we'll probably end up in Brooklyn some place and at the rate we're going, we will create quite a furore when we do get there."

"Why," asked Dolores, "what has our slow pace got to do with the hit we'll make, appearing in a subway station in Brooklyn attired only in our bathing suits?"

"Did you ever see three old ladies, or even one, climb up on the platform of a subway station, dressed in a torn and very abbreviated bathing suit?" Mabel giggled.

Just as Mabel finished speaking, a dull thud and a sharp cry from Dolores caused the other two to halt in alarm. Wrenching her hand free from Alice's grasp, Dolores sank to the floor and although the others could not see her, they heard her moan as though in pain. Dropping to the floor beside her, Mable and Alice quickly found the huddled form of the mysteriously stricken girl. Reaching out in the darkness, Alice touched the soft, dark mass of Dolores' hair but a sudden cry from the tall Camp Fire girl caused her to withdraw her exploring fingers quickly and in alarm.

"Dolores!" she cried anxiously, "speak to me! What's the matter? What happened?"

"Oooh!" moaned the prostrate Dolores, "my head! I just gave it an awful wallop against something hard! I think we've come to the end of the tunnel but we might be able to go further. According to the way my head feels, I must have butted a hole in this wall big enough to crawl through! Let's see if we can find out what I ran into. It felt wooden and sounded hollow. Maybe there's a door around here some place."

Rising to their feet, the three girls took a cautious step further, with arms outstretched. Another step and their groping fingers came in contact with rough boards. Feeling from the floor to as high as they could reach and from one end of the wall to the other, the girls were unable to find any trace of a door or any opening that would permit them to continue their explorations further. The left fork of the tunnel terminated in a blank wall and as Dolores again sank to the floor, holding her aching head between her hands, Mabel sighed and prepared to retrace her steps. Holding out both her hands to Alice and Dolores, she called to them to accompany her back.

"Come on," she said, resignedly, "there's no use in staying here any longer. We might as well go back and meet the others at the house or that place where we left them if they haven't had any more luck than we had. Gosh! The very thought of getting into that cold water again back there makes me shiver! Hurry up, let's get it over!"

"Wait a minute!" Alice suddenly cried as Dolores, rising again, took Mabel's hand. "I think I've found something! Come over here and help me with it. It's pretty heavy!"

Following the sound of Alice's voice in the darkness, Mabel and Dolores felt their way to where the petite, blonde Camp Fire girl was standing in an angle formed by the blank wall Dolores had struck her head against and one of the side walls. As Mabel bumped against her in the gloom, Alice took her hand and placed it over her head to where a large, metal object was fastened to the wall. Their fingertips just touched it but Dolores, who was taller than the rest, was able to place her entire hand against the metal. For a moment her fingers passed swiftly over the surface of the object and then, with a happy cry, she announced her discovery to her two friends.

"It's a bolt of some kind," she informed them excitedly, "and where there's a bolt there must be a door! I can't feel any hinges but I'm going to pull this bolt back just the same and see what happens. This whole wall must be a big door of some kind!"

Exerting all her strength, Dolores slid the heavy metal bar back in its groove but as the three anxiously waiting Camp Fire girls stood in the darkness expecting the door to swing back after pushing against it with all their might, they were doomed to disappointment for the wall remained where it was, as blank and as solid as ever.

"That's queer," murmured Alice perplexedly, "why should that bolt be there if not to hold a door shut? I know!" she suddenly shouted as an explanation occurred to her. "There must be another one on the other side! Come on, Dolores, you've got some more pushing to do yet before we get out of here. See if you can find another bolt at the other end of this wall."

Feeling their way in the darkness to the opposite side of the blank wall, Alice and Mabel followed Dolores until they suddenly bumped into her as she stopped. Raising her arm high above her head, Dolores passed her hand along the wall until her fingers came in contact with what they were seeking, the duplicate of the bolt Alice had discovered. Grasping the cold steel firmly in both hands, Dolores gave a sudden jerk but as she was about to aid Mabel and Alice in pushing against the wall again in an effort to swing it open, there was a rattling, scraping sound and as Mabel placed her hands against the rough boards, she felt them slip swiftly downward! The wall was sinking into the ground and as the girls waited in breathless amazement to see what would happen next, a gust of cold wind whipped around their bare arms and legs.

The rattling and scraping ceased with a dull thud and as Alice thrust her hands out before her she felt only the chilly air that was making the three Camp Fire girls shiver with cold. The wall had completely disappeared! Clasping hands again the three girls stepped into the inky blackness before them, not knowing what they would find. They had taken but a few steps forward when Mabel suddenly stopped.

"Smell anything?" she asked the others, sniffing the air around her. "I think we're in a garage or another boathouse. I smell burned gasoline and damp wood, don't you?"

"That's right," agreed Alice, also sniffing while Dolores followed their example, "I wish we had a light of some sort so we could see what kind of place this is."

"Those wheel tracks!" suddenly exclaimed Dolores. "Wait a minute, I have an idea!"

Dropping Mabel's hand, Dolores carefully felt her way in the darkness until her outstretched hands came in contact with a wall. Feeling her way along its side while Alice and Mabel stood in the darkness wondering what Dolores' idea could be, the tall Camp Fire girl's hand touched what she had hoped she would find. Pressing the button her reasoning had told her she would find some place in the darkness, all three startled girls blinked their eyes in the sudden blaze of light that sprang from the large bulb overhead.

Looking about them, the girls saw they were in a large room. Large packing cases were piled one on top of another all around them while bolted to the floor in the center of the room was a large, motor driven wheel around which was coiled a heavy steel cable. A strong wooden platform, mounted on ponderous steel wheels stood in front of it while a weighty iron hook, attached to one end of the cable lay on top of it. Instantly the alert girls read the explanation of the wheel ruts in the floor of the tunnel. They had been made by the steel wheels of the rolling platform as it was pulled through the tunnel from the boathouse by the cable, carrying the cases with which the room was almost filled from the motor boat to the store room in which they were now standing. As the girls pointed these facts out to one another, Mabel suddenly appeared from behind a packing case.

"This must be the end of the tunnel," she announced, "there's a ladder back there leading up to the roof. There's probably a trap door there. Let's see where it goes. Turn out the light, somebody, and let's go. I'm freezing to death here."

"But," protested Alice, "we've got to get that wall back in place before we leave. If we leave it like this, whoever comes here will know we've been here and our chances of catching these smugglers will be worth exactly nothing or much less."

"Maybe this will do the trick," announced Dolores, pointing to an electric switch near the button she had pressed a moment before. "Let's try it and see if it does."

Pushing the switch into place, Dolores grinned triumphantly as the wall rose up out of the ground and slid into place. Snapping off the light, Alice and Dolores followed the sound of Mabel's voice as she stood near the ladder and a moment later putting the full force of her weight behind it, Mabel pushed open the trap door in the ceiling. Pulling herself through the opening, Mabel turned and helped Alice and Dolores through. Surprised, the three girls found themselves in the open air and as they looked about them, trying to determine just where they were, Alice suddenly bent down and snatched something from the ground and held it aloft.

"We're still on the estate!" she cried in astonishment. "Look, here's one of those blue tiles Anita and I found this afternoon! We were going to dig here tomorrow!"

"Well, if we're so near the house," shivered Dolores, "let's hurry and go in. I'm stiff with cold. I wonder if the others are there yet? Do you think they found anything?"

"I don't know," replied Alice, closing the trap door, "but we'll soon find out."

Hurrying as fast as the rough ground on their bare feet would permit, the three girls hastened through the trees to the big house but when they arrived in the spacious living room, it was deserted. Their clothes were lying where they had left them when they changed into their bathing suits and they knew that if Mrs. Evans, Lenore and Anita had arrived ahead of them, they would have carried the garments upstairs. Relaxing in the warmth of the room, Alice, Mabel and Dolores were about to gather up the scattered clothes and take them upstairs when a sudden, scratching sound attracted their attention. Looking up, they followed the direction of the sound across the room and then suddenly their eyes grew round and they caught their breath in alarm as they saw the massive, carved mantelpiece slowly slide into the wall!

CHAPTER VII

Waiting until Dolores, Alice and Mabel had disappeared into the darkness of the left fork of the tunnel, Mrs. Evans, beckoning to Lenore and Anita, turned and plunged into the gloom of the right branch of the subterranean passage. Feeling their way carefully, placing one bare foot gingerly before the other on the rough boards of the floor, the two Camp Fire girls and their leader moved slowly through the inky darkness. Both branches of the tunnel were of approximately the same length and width and since the three Federal Investigators in each tunnel moved forward at the same slow pace because of the absolute darkness surrounding them, Mrs. Evans, Anita and Lenore tripped and fell heavily almost at the same time that Dolores bumped her head against the sliding wall in the left branch of the passage.

Groping about in the darkness, the Camp Fire Guardian and the two girls found they had tripped over the first step of a short flight of stairs leading upward and rather than incur the risk of falling again, the three Federal Investigators mounted the stairway on their hands and knees. Reaching out in the gloom for the next step, Mrs. Evans, who was in the lead, found that she had arrived at the top of the flight. Still kneeling, she turned around and whispered to the two behind her.

"I'm at the top," she announced. "There are only a few steps. Stand up and walk."

As Lenore and Anita, obeying their leader's instructions and reached the landing on which she was standing, the three joined hands and continued on their way. They had not gone far, however, when Lenore's outstretched hand came in contact with something solid that barred their progress. The three were walking abreast and while Lenore held her hand out in front of her, Mrs. Evans felt along the wall next to her. Anita, being in the middle, was occupied with holding the free hands of Lenore and her leader. Stopping when Lenore stopped, Mrs. Evans and Anita both spoke at the same time, asking the same question of the red-haired Camp Fire girl.

"What's the matter?" they whispered. "Did you hear something? Is some one coming?"

"No," replied Lenore, smiling in the darkness as her hand passed over the obstruction in their way, "I haven't heard anything, but I think I've found something that feels as though it might be a door but I can't find the doorknob. Maybe it's over on your side. We're standing right in front of it. See if you can find it over there."

Mrs. Evans' search, however, was as fruitless as Lenore's and as the three Federal Investigators stood in the darkness, their path blocked by what Lenore was certain was a door, Anita raised her foot and placing it against the barrier, threw the full force of her weight behind it. A creaking, rasping sound echoed through the dark silence of the tunnel and Anita uttered an exultant shout as she felt the obstruction give way before her. Lowering her foot, she tugged at the hands she held.

"Come on!" she cried. "I've pushed your old door open, let's see what's behind it!"

But as the three investigators took a confident step forward, expecting to pass through the opening, they found their way still blocked by the same obstruction.

"I thought you said you opened this door or whatever it is," exclaimed Lenore reproachfully, rubbing a bruised knee tenderly. "You must be imagining things."

"But I'm sure I felt it swing open when I pushed it," protested Anita, "and besides you heard the hinges squeak as well as I did. Let's try it again, all together."

"That won't be necessary," replied Mrs. Evans, "I think I've solved the mystery. This is evidently a swinging door and the springs are so rusty that Anita's push only opened the door a trifle and of course, as soon as she took her foot away, the door swung back into place. I think I can push it open myself and then you can follow me through. I wonder what this tunnel is being, or has been, used for?"

Turning around, the Camp Fire leader placed her back against the door and bracing her feet on the rough boards of the floor, slowly pushed the door back while Anita and Lenore, each holding one of her hands, followed her across the threshold. The tunnel seemed to continue beyond the door since the two Camp Fire girls and their leader found themselves surrounded by the same impenetrable darkness as before.

As they took a hesitating step forward, Lenore suddenly stopped and slid one bare foot experimentally across the floor. Since the three had joined hands again after passing through the door, Anita and Mrs. Evans stopped with her, but in surprise.

"What's the matter?" asked Anita. "Did you find another door or are you tired?"

"Neither," replied Lenore. "Rub your foot along the floor. Notice anything different?"

As Mrs. Evans and Anita followed Lenore's instructions, they found to their delight and surprise that the floor on which they were standing was now made of smooth, finished boards instead of the rough, uneven planks over which they had been walking. The portion of the tunnel in which they found themselves also seemed to be warmer than the section through which they had just passed. Stretching out her arm to feel for the wall as a guide in order to continue on their way, Mrs. Evans was unable to feel anything, nor was Lenore, when, at her leader's request, she too groped in the darkness for a wall. Thinking that perhaps the tunnel became wider at that particular point, Mrs. Evans, releasing her hand from Anita's, took a few steps to her left, instructucting Lenore to follow the same procedure to her right.

A sudden crash and a startled cry from Lenore caused Anita, who was standing alone where Mrs. Evans and Lenore had left her, to leap forward in fright and a second later she too cried out but in triumph rather than alarm as her body collided with some heavy, solid object and her hands shot out in the darkness, seeking what she hoped they would find. In the meantime, Mrs. Evans, whirling about at the sudden commotion, hurried forward in the inky blackness to render what assistance she could to the two girls. She had taken but a few steps, however, when a sudden glow of light pierced the darkness and Anita rose triumphantly from her half crouching position while Lenore lay on the floor, trying to disentangle herself from the chair over which she had fallen. Looking about them in amazement, the three Federal Investigators saw they were in a small room, equipped as an office. The light that illuminated their surroundings came from a lamp on the desk against which Anita had inadvertently hurled herself and Mrs. Evans took a hasty backward step as she saw that another few inches would have precipitated her against the steel side of a filing cabinet. The desk was littered with papers and as the three investigators bending over, examined them, Mrs. Evans gasped with surprise as the full import of their contents became apparent to her. With shining eyes, she turned to Lenore and Anita, pointing with a trembling finger to the papers scattered over the desk.

"Evidence!" she exulted. "We've got something to report to Mr. Baldwin at last! These papers are orders for and records of smuggled goods! This room is probably the smugglers' headquarters! Come on, we've got to get back to the house as quickly as we can and phone Mr. Baldwin. We can't stay here long anyhow. Those men might return at any minute! Turn off the light. We can't afford to be caught just yet!"

While Mrs. Evans was speaking, Anita had turned her attention to the filing cabinet and was endeavoring to pull open its drawers. They were locked, however, but as she tugged, she dislodged a large globe placed on top of it. Picking it up, she was about to return it to its place when something on the wall immediately above the cabinet attracted her attention. The object appeared to be a small design carved in the wood work and reaching up, Anita touched it. It moved beneath her fingers and at the same instant the wall immediately to the left of it began to slide away!

With a startled cry, Anita stepped back just as Mrs. Evans switched off the desk lamp and together the three stood in the darkness watching a narrow slit of light grow wider and wider as the wall slid further and further away. Suddenly Anita gasped and Lenore and Mrs. Evans started forward as the opening became wide enough for them to see into the room beyond. The lamplight that provided the illumination revealed familiar surroundings and as Lenore, Anita and Mrs. Evans stepped through the opening that had slowly become wide enough to permit them to pass, three very frightened Camp Fire girls breathed great sighs of relief and two Camp Fire girls and their leader looked about them in surprise. Suddenly all six burst into peals of merry laughter at the ludicrous picture they presented to one another. Their arms, legs and faces scratched and covered with dirt, their bathing suits torn and covered with grime, the six Federal Investigators stood in the living room of the mansion on Long Island Sound and hastily compared notes of their discoveries.

"Golly! You had us scared green when you pushed that fireplace back," laughed Mabel. "What did you find? We discovered the place where those smugglers are hiding their stuff and we know how it gets there. All we have to do now is get them."

"Mr. Baldwin will take care of that," replied Mrs. Evans. "We found their records which is evidence enough, but with what you've found, I don't think Mr. Baldwin will have any trouble in successfully putting an end to their activities. I'm going to phone him now. The rest of you see if you can get that mantlepiece back into place."

The girls soon found the hidden button, similar to the one Anita discovered on the other side of the wall and as the massive, oak fixture slid back into its normal position, Alice began gathering up her clothes, the others following her example.

"All I want now," she announced as she went upstairs, "is a nice, hot bath, some iodine and a pair of tweezers. I'm so full of splinters, I feel like a pine tree."

Reaching their bedrooms, each with its own private bath, the girls were soon relaxing in their tubs. Although it had seemed much longer, their exploration of the tunnel had taken little more than an hour and as the five Camp Fire girls and their leader completed their ablutions, they gathered as had become their habit, in Mrs. Evans' room to finish dressing. It was too early to go to bed and the six Federal Investigators were too excited over their new discoveries to sleep, especially since Mrs. Evans told them that Mr. Baldwin was on his way out to Long Island, after receiving her telephone message, with men from his office to apprehend the smugglers.

Instead of going downstairs again after completing their toilettes, Mrs. Evans and the five girls took their binoculars and, mounting the stairs to the third floor, entered the large room shared by Alice and Lenore. For some time they watched the tossing waves and flashing beams of the lighthouse, hoping to catch a glimpse of the mysterious motor boat as it entered or left the long, low boathouse on the beach. As the minutes ticked slowly by, Mrs. Evans was about to declare the vigil fruitless when Dolores suddenly uttered a sharp exclamation as she focused her glasses on a distant point, calling the others' attention to what she saw there.

"There's a boat!" she announced. "Beyond the lighthouse! I can see its lights."

Snapping on a small reading lamp near Alice's bed, Mrs. Evans unfolded a newspaper clipping she had been holding in her hand and consulted it and as the others looked over her shoulder, they saw it was a schedule of steamship arrivals and sailings that their leader had torn from that day's newspaper before dinner.

"Let's see," she mused, scanning the columns and referring to her wrist watch, "today is the twenty-fourth and it's just ten thirty. Evidently that boat is the 'Carpathia' and according to this schedule, the 'Ambassador' is due in about half an hour. Watching ocean liners steam into Long Island Sound is a very pretty sight," she concluded, switching off the light, "but it doesn't help us any. I don't think we'll see anything of those smugglers tonight. Let's go downstairs and wait for Mr. Baldwin. We can show him what we've found and he can have his men wait in that underground room and in the office behind the fireplace for the smugglers."

Mabel was the last of the six to reach the enormous living room and as she limped in behind the others, she sank into the first chair she came to with a great sigh.

"My feet are killing me," she moaned. "These are new shoes and I left the most comfortable pair I own on the beach. Who wants to come down with me while I get them?"

"I'll go," volunteered Dolores. "My head still aches from that bump I gave it in the tunnel and a little fresh air might help. We'd better get them all anyway because if those smugglers find them there, so near the boathouse, they might become suspicious and not return. I've got a flashlight in my bag. I'll get it and then we'll go. The rest of you can wait here for Mr. Baldwin, if you want to."

"That's a good idea," agreed Mrs. Evans, "but hurry right back. It's getting late."

Obtaining her flashlight, Dolores and Mabel set off for the beach while Mrs. Evans, Lenore, Alice and Anita settled themselves to wait for Mr. Baldwin and the group of Federal agents he was bringing with him to the old Dutton estate.

CHAPTER VIII

Returning to the boathouse with the power launch, the two men whose voices the girls and Mrs. Evans heard while standing waist deep in the water covered by the low shack, growled at one another, blaming each other for the error that had sent them out needlessly and without lights on a short cruise up the Sound. As the nose of the boat bumped softly against the large double doors, one of them held his hand up in a terse command for silence while the other looked at him questioningly.

"Sh!" commanded the first man. "Be quiet! I think I hear some noise in there."

"Ramon, my friend," sneered the other after listening a moment, "you are a fool. There is no noise in there other than the lapping of the waves. Open the doors."

It was then that Mrs. Evans and the five girls swam swiftly and silently back to the movable platform that marked the beginning of the tunnel they subsequently explored. The two men, unaware of the presence of the six Federal Investigators, secured the boat to its moorings within the boathouse and stepping out on the platform beneath which Mrs. Evans and the girls were hiding, unlocked the small back door and set off along the beach in the general direction of the village. Returning some hours later, one of the men suddenly seized the other's arm and pointed excitedly at a dancing ray of light ahead of them. The other laughed.

"Again, Ramon," he scoffed, "you are a fool. A flashlight in the hands of a girl is no cause for alarm. We shall wait until they have gone and then continue ourselves."

Arriving at the beach, Mabel and Dolores, with the aid of the flashlight, began looking for the six pairs of shoes they knew were somewhere in the vicinity of the boathouse and it was while they were searching for them that the two men saw the beams of the flashlight in Mabel's hand. Standing where they were, the black shadows of the night concealing them from view, the men waited until Mabel and Dolores should quit the beach but unaware of the fact that they were being watched, the two Camp Fire girls discussed the recent events of the evening.

Complete silence reigned all about them and so it was not difficult for the two men standing nearby to overhear all that was said. With a sudden snarl the man who had first seen the pencil line of light made by the flashlight whirled on his companion, his hand flying instinctively to his belt from which hung a knife.

"So, Manuel," he hissed, "it is I who am the fool, not once but twice. You have heard what I have heard. Prepare to pay for your blundering with your worthless life."

"Softly, Ramon, my hot headed one," soothed

Manuel. "The senoritas undoubtedly have keen ears and many friends nearby. The evening is warm, the night is dark and the waters are deep and so two senoritas who went for a swim, never returned, alas!"

"Manuel," grinned the other in the darkness, "I apologize. You are a genius and I await your command. Senor X will commend us highly for this night's work, amigo."

Their footsteps muffled by the deep sand and their approach masked by the inky blackness, the two men crept silently forward as Dolores and Mabel, bending over, were gathering up the six pairs of shoes they had been looking for. Mabel had removed the pair she was wearing and was about to replace them with the more comfortable pair while Dolores stood waiting for her when suddenly they felt themselves seized from behind while rough hands covered their mouths! The arms that held them were strong and although the two Camp Fire girls struggled with all the strength at their command, they were no match for the two men who easily overpowered them. Still struggling and kicking, Dolores and Mabel were carried to the boathouse and while one of the men unlocked the door with his free hand, the other, who was holding Mabel, reached out and seized Dolores as well lest she manage to escape while her antagonist was occupied in opening the boathouse door.

Forcing the two girls into the boat, the men swiftly bound and gagged them and while one pushed the front doors open, the other, picked up a long pole, and began propelling the boat out of the boathouse much in the manner of a Venetian gondolier. As Dolores and Mabel watched them from the bottom of the boat, they knew why they had never heard the throb of its engine as the big power launch came and went on its mysterious trips. Waiting until they were some distance from shore, the men finally started the powerful motor and as the boat sped through the night, the two Camp Fire girls noticed that they were travelling without lights, which, they knew, was another reason why they had never seen the boat come and go as they had watched for it with their binoculars.

While the men occupied themselves with steering the craft through the dark waters, Mabel and Dolores struggled with their bonds. The cords cut deep into Mabel's excess flesh but Dolores was slim and able, by dint of much hard work, to loosen the bonds around her wrists. Slowly and carefully pushing herself to a semi-sitting position, she was able to exert more strength against her ropes and a moment later she managed to get one hand free. Snatching the handkerchief from her mouth, she freed her other hand and then rolling over, began loosening the cords that held Mabel prisoner. Rubbing their numbed wrists and ankles, the girls peered cautiously over the side of the boat.

Looking about them, Dolores and Mabel saw they were lying in the stern of the boat while their two captors were standing in the prow. The engine had been shut off and as the boat drifted aimlessly on the Sound, the girls saw that each of the two men held a long pole in his hand. Suddenly one of the men said something to the other in a low voice and as he turned around to start the engine again, both Mabel and Dolores crouched low in order to avoid being seen. The roar of the engine and the rapid staccato of its exhaust told the girls the boat was under way again and as the vessel slipped swiftly through the water, Dolores raised her head to see where they were going. One quick glance was sufficient and as she crouched down beside Mabel, she whispered a plan of escape that met with speedy approval.

"I just saw the lights of an ocean liner ahead of us," she whispered. "It's the 'Ambassador' that Mrs. Evans said was due half an hour after the 'Carpathia.' They are evidently going to wait until it's out of sight before they get rid of us but we can jump overboard when we get near enough to the 'Ambassador' and be picked up by them. I think there's a pilot boat that meets all liners here in the Sound someplace, so if we can't attract the attention of the liner's crew, we certainly ought to be able to signal the pilot boat if it's around here any place now."

As Dolores whispered her plan to Mabel, they felt the boat slacken its speed and as they raised themselves up carefully, ready to carry out their plan, they saw the massive hulk of the ocean liner loom up in the darkness ahead of them. Just as they were about to lower themselves into the water in order to avoid making a splash and thus attract unwanted attention from their captors, they heard a splash followed by two others in rapid succession. The lights from the big ship cast enough illumination on the waters around them to enable them to see what made the noise and as the two men, again standing in the prow of the boat lunged forward with their long poles, Mabel and Dolores smothered a gasp of surprise as they saw what was happening. Large bales were being thrown from an opening in the ship's side and as they struck the water near the power launch, the two men seized them with their poles, hauled them alongside and pulled them aboard! The ocean liner was slowly moving away and as the men lifted the last bale from the water, Mabel and Dolores seized their fleeting opportunity and slipped swiftly into the water. Swimming rapidly along the side of the slowly moving ocean greyhound, the girls refrained from shouting for aid lest their captors hear them and re-capture them. Swimming ahead of Mabel, Dolores suddenly struck her hand against something protruding from the ship's side and as she grasped it, she felt herself being pulled along by it. Turning to Mabel, she held out her other hand, pulling her up next to her.

"Quick!" she gasped, "I've caught hold of the pilot's ladder! Give me your hand before the boat gets away from us! We've got to get aboard and find the captain!"

With their last remaining ounce of strength, the girls pulled themselves up the ladder at the ship's side and a moment later tumbled over the railing onto the deck. For a few minutes they lay where they were, unnoticed by anyone, slowly regaining their strength. Just as Dolores was about to rise, footsteps coming along the deck in their direction caused both girls to shrink back into the dark shadows, since they did not wish to be observed by any of the passengers aboard. A light from a nearby window, however, fell on the blue, gold braided uniform of a ship's officer and as he approached, both girls sprang to their feet in front of him. Completely taken by surprise, the officer whipped a gun from his pocket but a second later he dropped it in astonishment as he took notice of the two bedraggled figures before him. Looking from one to the other, he finally managed to speak.

"What is the meaning of this?" he demanded. "Who are you and why are you so wet?"

"Are you the captain?" asked Mabel. "We've got to see him at once. It's important!"

"I'll take you to the captain," promised the officer sternly, "but wait until your parents hear of this! What is your stateroom number and what are your names?"

"We just got on board," explained Dolores meekly as the officer led them along the deck. "We were swimming in the sound and when this boat came along, we just got on."

Sputtering indignantly, the officer knocked on a door at the end of a corridor within the ship and receiving a muffled invitation to enter, opened the portal and ushered the girls into the presence of the captain of the ocean liner, explaining how and where he found them. For a moment the amazed captain was speechless but Dolores and Mabel gave him no chance to question them. As quickly and as briefly as they could, they told him what they had just seen and the circumstances leading up to their presence on the boat. At the mention of Mr. Baldwin's name, the captain waited to hear no more. With a roar that sounded like an angry lion, he leaped from his chair and began hurling orders at the astonished officer in terse commands.

"I'll soon put a stop to such goings on aboard my ship!" he stormed. "Take some men and go down to the hold! I don't care if you have to arrest every man in the crew! I'll soon find out who is responsible for this! Radio the nearest Coast Guard station to be on the lookout for those men in the power launch and send a stewardess here to take care of these young ladies! Get going! Time is valuable!"

The two shivering Camp Fire girls were soon provided with warm, dry clothes and as they sat in the captain's office drinking the hot cocoa the stewardess brought them, the door opened and two officers entered, pushing four rough looking, burly fellows before them, all securely handcuffed to one another with heavy chains.

"Here they are, sir," announced one of the officers. "They've confessed everything. They work for a smuggling gang in New York. They get their goods included in a ship's cargo and then toss it overboard in Long Island Sound where other members of the gang pick it up and dispose of it. If it weren't for these young ladies, we never would have caught them, since somehow or other, they managed things very cleverly."

"Put them in the brig and turn them over to the Customs officials when we dock!" commanded the captain and then turning to Dolores and Mabel, he held out his hand in congratulation.

"Good work, girls," he smiled, "and I'm glad to know you're Camp Fire girls. My daughter has been asking me to let her join and believe me, she's going to, too, as soon as I get home to give my consent. I'm sorry I can't take you back to Long Island, but I'll see that you get quick transportation out there as soon as we dock, which should be in about forty-five minutes at the latest."

"Isn't there same way we can get word to the others?" asked Mabel. "They'll be wondering what happened to us and if they go down to the beach to look for us, they might run into those same men or more of their gang! We ought to warn them."

"I'll send another message to the Coast Guard station," promised the captain, "and ask them to send some men ashore with your message. They might be able to help capture the others, too, while they're there, all thanks to your good work tonight."

As the captain left his office to dispatch his second message to the Coast Guard station, a swift, grey cutter turned about in its course and sped swiftly along Long Island Sound in response to the first radio message received from the "Ambassador" and as the second message flashed through the air, its powerful searchlight swept the waters of Long Island Sound.

CHAPTER IX

As Mrs. Evans, Alice, Lenore and Anita waited in the living room of the big house for Mr. Baldwin, the Camp Fire leader kept glancing from time to time at her watch. Finally, with an impatient gesture, she rose from her chair and began pacing up and down the room while the three girls watched her perplexedly for it was not like their Camp Fire Guardian to exhibit signs of nervousness or apprehension. Looking at her watch again, she crossed the room to where Lenore and Anita were sitting.

"I don't know what can be keeping Mabel and Dolores so long," she said. "They've been gone over half an hour and it only takes a few minutes at the most to go down to the beach and back again. I'm going to see if I can find them."

"We'll go with you," chorused the three girls at once rising, but Mrs. Evans shook her head and pointed to her wrist watch while the three girls looked at theirs.

"Mr. Baldwin will be here any minute now," the Camp Fire leader replied, "and some one should be here when he arrives. I'll only be gone a minute or two and if Mr. Baldwin should come while I'm gone, ask him to wait for me. I'll be right back."

"I'm going with you," announced Alice firmly as

Mrs. Evans prepared to leave the house. "Lenore and Anita can wait for Mr. Baldwin and keep him here until we return."

In the meantime, Ramon and Manuel, having hauled the last bale aboard the power launch, turned to devote their attentions to Mabel and Dolores. Finding only the cords that had held them, both men shrugged their shoulders and turned the boat back toward the beach where they knew others would soon be waiting for them to land.

"It was very thoughtful of the senoritas to drown themselves and save us the trouble," Manuel mused as he guided the boat back to the boathouse. "No person can swim long in the powerful undertow of Long Island Sound, Ramon, my friend."

Expecting momentarily to meet Dolores and Mabel, Mrs. Evans and Alice reached the beach but only the lapping of the waves and the long, white stretch of sand greeted them. Ramon and Manuel had already anchored the boat in the boathouse and as they waited for the other members of their lawless band to arrive, they were unaware of the presence of Mrs. Evans and Alice just outside the windowless shack. As the Camp Fire girl and her leader approached the boathouse, Alice stepped on something hard and as she bent down to see what it was, she uttered a small cry of alarm as she picked up and recognized Dolores' flashlight. A few paces further on, they found the shoes. A hasty count by Mrs. Evans revealed that there were seven instead of six pair, indicating that Mabel was unshod when she disappeared, since two pair were easily identified as hers. So alarmed were the Camp Fire leader and Alice over the discovery that they failed to notice the approach of several men until one of them seized Mrs. Evans roughly by the arm while another snatched the torch from Alice.

"What're you doing here?" demanded Mrs. Evans' captor. "Don't you know this is my private property? I'll give both of you just five minutes to get off the premises."

Mrs. Evans, however, was not so easily intimidated. Wrenching her arm free from the man's grasp, she whirled and faced her antagonist coolly while Alice gripped two high heeled shoes, one in each hand, ready and on the alert for instant action.

"Who are you?" demanded the courageous Camp Fire Guardian evenly, "and what are you doing here? I happen to know that this is not private property. Let us pass."

"Pretty spunky, aren't you?" sneered the man. "O.K., I'll give you something to be spunky about!" and turning to the small group of men behind him, he continued.

"You men get to work, Mike and I will handle these inquisitive young ladies alone!"

Waiting until the others had entered the boathouse, the two men approached Alice and Mrs. Evans but they were ready for them. Springing to instant action, Alice lashed out with both shoes while Mrs. Evans, bending double, bowled over her adversary by the simple expedient of butting him in the middle. Several resounding thwacks followed by startled grunts gave ample evidence of the effective use to which Alice was putting her high heeled weapons, while Mrs. Evans, leaping upon the prone form of her fallen foe, sent her small but hard fists crashing again and again into her adversary's face. The sudden and altogether unexpected attack from the two courageous Federal Investigators had taken the men by surprise but their astonishment soon gave way to seething anger and as they brought their superior weight and strength into play, Mrs. Evans and Alice saw they were waging a hopeless battle. Although they fought valiantly, the Camp Fire girl and her leader were overpowered and carried, still kicking and scratching, into the boathouse. Just as their captors were entering the windowless shack, however, the powerful rays of a marine searchlight picked them out of the darkness and a second later three forms were wading through the water toward the beach. Unaware of their approach, the two men bound and gagged their prisoners and dumping them unceremoniously into the power launch, began directing the work of unloading. In the meantime, Mr. Baldwin and his men had arrived at the old mansion where Anita and Lenore explained to them all that they had discovered.

As the minutes passed and the missing Federal Investigators still did not return, Lenore's anxiety prompted a suggestion.

"I don't know what could have happened to them," she began, "unless they were caught by those smugglers. Maybe it would be a good idea if we went through the tunnel again. Anita could lead some of you through the part that ends behind the fireplace and I'll show the others where all that machinery is under that blue tile border. If nothing else, we'll at least save time and be doing something besides just waiting but I think the others are in trouble, since they've been gone so long."

Accepting Lenore's suggestion, the men divided themselves into two groups, one going with Lenore to the space marked off by the blue tile border while the others followed Anita as she stepped through the opening left by the sliding mantelpiece.

Aboard the "Ambassador", their clothes dried and neatly pressed, Mabel and Dolores waited anxiously for the ship to dock. Never had the comparatively brief span of forty-five minutes seemed so long to the two girls as they impatiently paced the deck of the ocean liner and watched the blur of lights that marked New York's sky line grow gradually brighter and clearer as the ship nosed her way to its dock.

"I think this ship is standing still!" wailed Mabel looking over the side. "I bet we haven't moved two inches since we've been on board! Mrs. Evans will be frantic!"

"We're moving, all right," replied Dolores, "but if we went any slower, we would be standing still. I hope the Coast Guard boat catches those two men before they find out we've escaped. They might go back and discover the others before help arrives."

"I beg your pardon, ladies," suddenly came a voice from the darkness behind them and as Dolores and Mabel whirled around, they saw one of the ship's officers rapidly approach them. "The captain wishes me to inform you," he continued, "that he has been in communication, by radio, with the Customs officers in New York. They are sending a seaplane alongside to pick you up and take you back to Long Island. Mr. Baldwin is already on his way out there but we have had no word from the Coast Guard cutter as yet. The plane will be here in a few minutes and you will probably be landed on the beach near your house within five minutes after taking off."

"Great!" cried Mabel. "Now we're getting some action! We'll be back in time to warn the others and identify those two men if Mr. Baldwin succeeds in capturing them."

"But how can we identify them?" asked Dolores. "We didn't get a chance to see their faces or their clothes or anything and even if we had, it was too dark to make sure."

"I can identify them by their voices," replied Mabel. "Didn't you notice their foreign accents? And I know one of them had a moustache because I pulled it!"

As Dolores was about to reply, the attention of the girls was attracted by the roar of an aeroplane motor as it swooped down from the sky and circled the steamship.

"There's our plane!" cried Mabel. "Come on, let's go! We haven't any time to waste!"

While a powerful searchlight from the boat cast a bright illumination on the big seaplane as it settled gracefully on the water near the ship, the girls were led down the ladder by which they had boarded the ocean liner a short while before. A row boat, manned by two sailors was waiting for them and in a few seconds they were climbing aboard the government amphibian.

Racing at a low altitude over the waters of Long Island Sound, the pilot pointed the nose of his plane toward the Long Island shore and a few minutes later the roar of the motors suddenly stopped as he shut off his ignition and landed his plane near a gleaming expanse of beach.

"I don't know how near we are to where you want to go," he called back to Dolores and Mabel from his cockpit, "but if this isn't it, we can scout around until we do find it. Do you recognize any familiar landmarks on the beach or is it too dark?"

"It is rather dark to see much," replied Dolores, "but I don't think this is it."

"I know it isn't," answered Mabel. "The place we're looking for has a boathouse and a small pier at the water's edge and I don't see anything like that around here. I think it's up further, near the other end of Long Island some place."

"O.K.," replied the pilot, "we're not far from there. I'll just taxi through the water and you tell me where and when to stop. There's a searchlight in the nose of the plane but you can work it from here. We'll find the place quicker that way."

"Fine!" exclaimed Mabel climbing over the small partition between the two open cockpits. "I'll work the searchlight and you keep your eyes open for the boathouse, Lenore. Let's go! The others probably think we've been drowned or murdered by now!"

As the seaplane slipped through the dark, silent waters, Lenore, who was standing up in her cockpit in order to obtain a better view of the shore line as outlined by the rays from the powerful searchlight, suddenly shouted and pointed ahead of her.

"There it is!" she cried. "There's the boathouse but look, who are those people on the beach? Why, it looks like—it is! Oh my gracious!" she almost screamed, "hurry, hurry! Please hurry! They've captured Mrs. Evans and Alice and maybe the others, too! They're carrying them into the boathouse! Oh whatever will we do? Haven't you a radio on this plane so we can send out an S.O.S. to the Coast Guard or somebody?"

"We don't need a radio," replied the pilot quietly. "I'll handle those beach bandits myself! You girls stay in the plane and keep it from drifting away. I'll be right back. If you don't hear from me in ten minutes, abandon ship and go for help."

"For an efficient pilot, you get some of the queerest ideas I ever heard," replied Mabel, stepping out on the low, broad wing of the plane. "Not only are we going to go with you but we're going to show you how to rescue our friends and not get shot."

Dolores had followed Mabel out on the wing of the plane and as both girls jumped into the shallow water and began wading to shore, the pilot threw out the small anchor with which his plane was equipped and followed suit.

Drawing a revolver from his pocket, the pilot at once raced toward the boathouse as soon as he set foot on the beach but Dolores, seeing what he was about to do, ran after him and caught him by the arm. Placing her finger to her lips, the Camp Fire girl led the surprised pilot away from the boathouse, lest her voice be heard by those inside.

"There are too many men in there for you to handle alone," she whispered, "and if you shoot, you're liable to hit some of the other girls or Mrs. Evans. Follow us."

As the three raced across the beach to the steps leading up to the roadway, Mabel and Dolores told the pilot about the tunnel leading from the boathouse. Their plan was to follow the tunnel from the old mansion to the boathouse and thus surprise their friends' abductors from behind, hoping that by the time they had effected the rescue, Mr. Baldwin and his men or the Coast Guardsmen or both would have arrived on the scene.

The traffic on the road above the beach had diminished and the three lost no time in reaching the gateway to the estate. Rousing Mr. Hawkins from his bed, they enlisted his aid, while Mrs. Hawkins phoned to the village.

"Maybe Lenore and Anita are still in the house," panted Dolores as they ran up the gravel walk to the big house. "I only saw Mrs. Evans and Alice on the beach just as they were being carried into the boathouse. I wonder why Mr. Baldwin hasn't arrived yet? Do you suppose he came and not finding anyone here, went away again?"

"Hardly," gasped Mabel throwing open the front door of the mansion. "Hello!" she called as the little party burst into the house. "Anyone here? Lenore, Alice, where are you? Wohelo!" she cried, giving the signal that all Camp Fire girls know but only the muffled echoes reverberating from the high ceilings answered her and as she and Dolores ran from room to room, upstairs and down, both girls realized with sinking hearts that save for themselves, Sam Hawkins and the pilot, the house was deserted. Returning to the living room where Hawkins and the pilot were waiting, Dolores and Mabel dejectedly reported their failure to find the other girls.

In the meantime, Mrs. Evans and Alice were lying in the bottom of the power launch, bound and gagged by the same cords that had held Mabel and Dolores a short time before. While the smugglers busied themselves in unloading their craft, Mrs. Evans worked feverishly at her bonds but to no avail. Manuel and Ramon, having lost two captives before, were taking no chances and both Mrs. Evans and Alice found themselves so securely bound that their fingers and toes were becoming numb from the pressure of the ropes on their wrists and ankles. As the last bale was lifted from the boat and attached to the rolling platform at the end of the steel cable reaching the entire length of the tunnel, one of the men, a tall, rough voiced individual whom Mrs. Evans guessed was the leader of the band, ordered the others to follow it.

"Get going," he commanded, "we've got to get this stuff unpacked before dawn."

"But Senor," protested one of the men, "what about our prisoners? Should we leave them here unguarded, they might manage to escape. Unfortunately, we are not out in deep water now as we were when the other two so imprudently left our custody."

"You do as you're told!" snarled the leader. "Get in there and help the others unpack. Manuel did a better job of trussing up than you did. They won't get away and when we come back, I'll teach them not to go sticking their noses into other people's business. They'll envy the two that were drowned when I get through with them," he sneered, bending over to make sure the cords were still securely tied.

At the mention of the two who were supposedly drowned, Mrs. Evans and Alice fought to restrain the tears of rage and sorrow that blurred their vision for they knew the men referred to Dolores and Mabel and unaware that the two girls had seen the capture of herself and Alice, Mrs. Evans reproached herself bitterly for having allowed them to go to the beach alone after dark without adequate protection. As the last of their captors disappeared into the black entrance of the tunnel, Mrs. Evans, redoubled her efforts to free herself but the more she struggled, the deeper the cords cut into her already bleeding flesh. Alice had ceased her struggles to free herself

Coast Guard cutter C-17. Pull along side, we've got you covered!"

"We've been looking for you!" shouted Mrs. Evans jubilantly as Alice shut off the engine. "We want to board you! Stand by to turn about and put on full steam ahead!"

CHAPTER X

As Mr. Baldwin and the four men he had chosen to accompany him stepped through the opening in the wall behind the fireplace, Anita touched the button releasing the secret spring and the huge mantelpiece slid noiselessly back into place again. It required no explanation from the Camp Fire girl to tell Mr. Baldwin what the desk and the filing cabinet contained. Swiftly and efficiently the men emptied the desk drawers and, forcing the lock on the cabinet, seized the records and papers with which it was filled.

Although the arrival of the smugglers was momentarily expected, Mr. Baldwin could not resist the temptation to glance through the pile of papers that was heaped up on the desk before him, all of which bore eloquent testimony to the practices engaged in by the lawless band.

"There's enough evidence here," he chuckled, leafing over the documents, "to send the whole outfit to jail for the rest of their lives, provided they don't get away from us. Murdock," he concluded, turning to one of the men, "I want you to take this stuff into New York at once. We can't afford to take the risk of losing it, now that we finally have something tangible to work on. Have Cassidy put it in my office safe and you stay there and guard it. Don't leave the office until I come back."

Gathering up the papers, Murdock waited until the mantelpiece had slid back far enough to allow him to pass through and as he left the old mansion, Anita returned the massive fixture to its original position again while Mr. Baldwin continued his examination of the room. Finding nothing more of importance, he turned to Anita.

"Now, where's this tunnel you were telling us about?" he asked and as Anita opened the door leading to the subterranean passage, the men produced their flashlights.

"Perhaps we had better not use those," Anita suggested, indicating the flashlights. "If those smugglers should return while we were going through the tunnel, those two flashlights would make excellent targets. Just follow me, I know the way in the dark."

"That's a good idea," agreed Mr. Baldwin as the two men returned their electric torches to their pockets. "Come on, let's go. I wonder if the others have had any luck?"

Switching off the light over the desk, Mr. Baldwin and the two men followed Anita into the dark recesses of the tunnel. Walking with more confidence, now that she knew where she was going, Anita proceeded swiftly along the dark passage, Mr. Baldwin and his assistants following closely at her heels. Keeping close to one wall of the tunnel, Anita occasionally reached out and touched it so she would know, when it terminated, that she had reached the place where the two branches met.

Meanwhile Lenore, leading the rest of the men Mr. Baldwin had brought with him to the patch of ground marked off by the border of blue tiles, found the trap door cleverly concealed by the shrubbery. Pointing it out to the men, she stepped aside while one of them lifted the heavy door. For a moment they listened at the opening to make sure that the room below was unoccupied before descending into it but hearing no sounds, Lenore scrambled nimbly down the ladder leading to the room while the men followed her in swift succession. With a whispered command to the men to stay where they were lest they trip over something in the darkness and attract the attention of the smugglers who might be in the vicinity, Lenore carefully felt her way among the bales and packing cases with which the room was filled, past the huge steel drum on which the cable was wound, to the wall where the light switch was located. As the bright light from the large bulb above the big steel drum flooded the room, one of the men swiftly opened a small valise he had been carrying and while the others examined the contraband goods with which the room was filled, he removed the contents of his bag which Lenore saw, to her surprise, contained all the material necessary for taking photographs indoors. Setting up his camera and fitting a photoflash bulb to his flashlight case, the man began taking pictures of the room and everything that was in it, including the trap-door in the ground above them.

"Photographic evidence to be presented in court," explained one of the men as he noted Lenore's look of surprise. "We can't cart all of these cases and bales into the courtroom but we can show pictures of them which will be accepted as evidence."

"In that case," replied Lenore, "you might as well take a picture of this, too," and crossing the room, she pulled open an electric switch not far from the light switch. As the wall thus released began sinking into the ground, the photographer took a picture of it while Lenore explained to the men what lay beyond that panel.

Re-packing his equipment, the photographer picked up his bag and followed Lenore as she led the men into the long, dark tunnel toward the boat-house. Arriving at the fork in the tunnel, Lenore suddenly stopped as the sound of approaching footsteps reached her ears. Not knowing if the noise were being made by Anita and Mr. Baldwin, in the other branch of the passage, or the smugglers returning to their den, Lenore whispered to those behind her to hold themselves in readiness for action while she attempted to discover the identity of those who were approaching. Standing at the entrance to the branch of the tunnel through which she had just passed, Lenore cupped her hands to her mouth and spoke in a low, soft voice, barely audible to those behind her.

"Wohelo!" she called, under her breath and

waited, tense and alert, for an answer. For a moment there was silence and Lenore began to regret her haste in revealing her presence in the tunnel but a second later an answering whisper came from the other branch of the passageway and the red-haired Camp Fire girl darted forward in the darkness to meet Anita as she and Mr. Baldwin emerged from the tunnel's left fork.

As the two Camp Fire girls and Mr. Baldwin and his men met in the darkness in front of the two branches of the tunnel, they paused for a moment and listened for any sound that would indicate the approach of the smugglers but only the soft rush of wind as it blew up the dark passageway from the boathouse reached their ears. Mr. Baldwin was about to command his men to move forward, with Lenore and Anita bringing up the rear, since the silence told them the coast was clear when suddenly a faint, muffled sound reached the keen ears of both Camp Fire girls. Their eyes had become sufficiently accustomed to the darkness to enable them to make out the dim forms of the men about them and as Mr. Baldwin was about to lead his men through the rest of the tunnel, Lenore, who was standing nearest him, reached out and grasped his arm.

"Wait a minute," she whispered. "I'm pretty sure I heard a noise coming from the other end of the tunnel just now. Maybe the smugglers are coming back! Listen!"

Borne by the wind which swept through the tunnel, the faint but unmistakable sounds of people moving about reached the ears of the twelve Federal officers as they stood listening at the end of the tunnel. Manuel and Ramon had returned, without Mabel and Dolores but in their place Alice and Mrs. Evans were being dumped roughly into the bottom of the boat. Unaware of what was going on below them, Mr. Baldwin waved his men back, directing some of them to return to the two rooms at the end of both branches of the tunnel while the others he placed in various strategic positions near the entrances of the two forks. As the men were about to carry out his orders, the sound of footsteps approaching along the tunnel from the direction of the boathouse arrested their attention and a moment later the voices of two men were heard.

"The boss says there's another load coming in on the 'Marius' tomorrow," said one.

"That means we'll have to get rid of this stuff tonight," replied the other, "or we won't have any room left when it does come in. We'll have to work fast."

As the men spoke, they emerged from the tunnel into the open space in which Mr. Baldwin and his men and Lenore and Anita were standing. No one moved and the two Camp Fire girls scarcely dared to breathe for fear some slight sound would reveal them to the two men, but totally unaware of their presence, the two smugglers went on, across the open space and into the branch of the tunnel which bore the wheel ruts on its floor.

As their voices and footsteps died in the distance,

Lenore and Anita breathed a faintly audible sigh of relief while Mr. Baldwin spoke to his men.

"We'll wait here now," he whispered, "until they begin unloading. The noise they'll make will cover our approach and we can take them by surprise. Get your camera ready, Davis. I want to get some pictures of them in actual operation before we stop them."

A sudden rumble and roar drowned out the photographer's whispered assent and a second later the flat, steel wheeled truck to which was attached one end of the cable flashed past them and vanished into the section of the tunnel leading to the boathouse. More noises followed as the men in the boat loaded the first of the heavy bales onto the truck while the two Camp Fire girls and Mr. Baldwin and his men watched the silver streak in the darkness that was the cable grow taut with the weight placed upon it. Suddenly the silence was broken by a whirring sound as the machinery that revolved the huge drum, coiling the cable around it, was put into motion. Slowly the silvery gleam of the cable retreated back through the tunnel while the wheels of the truck squealed and rumbled over the rough, wooden floor. Like some giant monster the girls saw a bale of contraband goods loom up out of the inky blackness of the tunnel and go swaying past them to disappear into the black maw of the tunnel's right fork. After a moment of silence, the heavy, flat truck with the cable, like a luminous tail attached to it, went streaking by again and again the watchers saw the cable grow tense and slide back into the darkness from which it came, pulling another large, unwieldy bale with it. Waiting until the massive bundle passed him, Mr. Baldwin was about to carry out his plan of photographing the smugglers at work while the rest of his men stood by, ready to thwart any attempts at escape when the sound of more voices and footsteps reached them!

As Lenore and Anita listened, with every sense alert, the sounds gradually grew nearer and nearer. Noiselessly darting from the entrance of one branch of the tunnel to the other, Anita listened carefully at each, returning to where Mr. Baldwin and Lenore were standing, with alarming news.

"Those footsteps and voices are coming from the left branch of the tunnel instead of from the right!" she announced. "There must be more men coming and from the sound of the footsteps there are more than two!"

* * * * * * * * * *

When Dolores and Mabel returned to the living room of the old mansion where Sam Hawkins and the seaplane pilot were waiting for them, Dolores threw herself down on a couch in utter despondency over Alice's and Mrs. Evans' capture and her failure to find Lenore and Anita anywhere in the house. Mabel, however, was made of sterner stuff. Pulling the disconsolate Dolores to her feet, she darted to the fireplace.

"Come on," she urged, "we've got to find the spring that releases this thing and get into that tunnel again somehow. We can reach the boathouse that way and maybe stop those smugglers before they take Alice and Mrs. Evans away from here. Hurry!"

Four pair of hands swiftly explored the surface of the old mantelpiece. Suddenly a metallic click was heard and the massive, handsomely carved fixture began to slide away from its original position. Too impatient to wait until the opening was big enough to allow them to pass through comfortably, the two Camp Fire girls, Hawkins and the pilot squeezed themselves through. Not stopping to notice the chaotic state in which Mr. Baldwin had left the room, Mabel and Dolores led the two men to the entrance to the tunnel and, taking the lead, plunged into the darkness before them.

Pressing themselves flat against the side walls, away from the three mouths of the tunnel, Lenore, Anita, Mr. Baldwin and his men waited to see who was approaching. Suddenly, as the heavy truck shot past them for the third time, a familiar voice reached the surprised ears of Anita and Lenore and a moment later the red-haired Camp Fire girl sprang to the entrance to the left branch of the tunnel with glee.

"Mabel, Dolores!" she whispered. "Where have you been? Who is that with you?"

As the four emerged from the fork of the tunnel, Lenore, Anita and Mr. Baldwin began hurling questions at Mabel and Dolores but Mabel cut all inquiries short.

"This is no time for talking!" she announced in a

crisp whisper. "We've got to rescue Alice and Mrs. Evans! They're being held prisoners by those smugglers down there in the boathouse! Come on, we've got to hurry before they take them away!"

"They won't have a chance!" replied Mr. Baldwin determinedly. "Curtis," he went on, "you and Riley go back and take those two smugglers in that room up there. You girls wait here for us. Come on, men, we've wasted enough time. Let's get this over with!"

"We're going with you," announced Lenore firmly but as she spoke the sound of several feet tramping through the tunnel again arrested their attention and they realized that, their work in the boathouse completed, the smugglers were coming toward them through the tunnel on their way to one or both rooms at the end of the forks! With sinking hearts, the four Camp Fire girls knew they were trapped!

CHAPTER XI

Steering the power launch alongside the Coast Guard cutter, Mrs. Evans and Alice were quickly taken aboard. A tall young man in a well fitting, blue uniform stood at the head of the companionway to greet them and as Mrs. Evans and Alice stepped aboard, he saluted smartly while a broad grin illuminated his handsome features, sharply outlined in the bright rays of the powerful searchlight. Introducing herself, Mrs. Evans began telling the young officer of the events that had just transpired but holding up one white gloved hand, the Coast Guardsman silenced the Camp Fire leader.

"We know all about you," he grinned; "in fact, we were out looking for you. It was very nice of you to come after us, however, because now you can show us the way to that boathouse and those smugglers of yours. Captain Erwin at your service, ma'm."

"But how did you find out about us?" asked the puzzled Camp Fire leader as she and Alice followed the captain to the bridge. "Did you receive a message from Mr. Baldwin?"

"No," replied the captain as he motioned to a sailor standing nearby to play the bright beams of the powerful Navy searchlight along the shore line, "we received a radio message from Captain Tremaine of the 'Ambassador'. He said two of your girls hopped a ride on his ship as it was going up the sound. Now," he went on, as the powerful rays of the searchlight cut a wide swath in the darkness, "which one of those shacks on the beach there is your boathouse or haven't we come to it yet?"

But Mrs. Evans and Alice were too overcome with joy to pay further attention to Captain Erwin just then for they knew that Mabel and Dolores had somehow escaped and were safe. As the Coast Guard cutter carrying the Camp Fire girl and her leader sped through the waters of Long Island Sound, Alice suddenly leaped forward as the searchlight picked the boathouse out of the inky darkness that surrounded them on the bridge.

"There it is!" she cried, pointing ahead of her. "There's the boathouse, captain!"

Instantly Captain Erwin began giving orders and a moment later a boat load of men was being lowered over the side, followed a second later by another boat containing Mrs. Evans, Alice and Lieutenant Graham in whose custody Captain Erwin had placed the two Federal Investigators while he took command of the landing party ashore. The big double doors of the boathouse were still swinging wide open as Mrs. Evans and Alice had left them when they made their escape a short while before and as the two row boats from the Coast Guard cutter were about to glide past them into the boathouse while the big searchlight illuminated its interior, a muffled sound of voices and stamping feet reached the occupants of the two row boats.

As soon as he heard the voices and footsteps of the smugglers approaching, Mr. Baldwin knew there was not a moment to lose. Curtis and Riley had already left to capture the two men who were operating the machinery in the room at the end of the right fork of the tunnel and so, grouping the remainder of his men, together with Sam Hawkins and the seaplane pilot, in a wide semi-circle in front of the mouth of the tunnel, Mr. Baldwin waited for the smugglers to walk into his trap. Revolvers and flashlights ready, the men stood on the alert for instant action while the four Camp Fire girls crouched in the entrance to the left branch of the tunnel. The silence, save for the slowly approaching voices and footsteps of the smugglers, was tense and strained. With nerves and muscles taut as steel wires drawn tight and eyes straining to peer through the darkness, the four Federal Investigators, Mr. Baldwin and the men waited what seemed to them an eternity. Suddenly Mabel's arm shot out in the darkness and caught Lenore's shoulder in a convulsive grasp while her other hand flew to her face but the gesture was too late to do any good. With a shuddering gasp, although she fought valiantly to suppress it, Mabel sneezed!

The sound shattered the silence like an explosion and Mr. Baldwin instantly took advantage of the momentary confusion and surprise he knew must be the smugglers'.

"Come on, men!" he shouted, his words ringing eerily through the tunnel, "let's go!"

But as he led his men in the charge down the tunnel, Mabel, Dolores, Anita and Lenore following close behind, the smugglers turned and fled, thinking to escape in the boat. The flashlights in the hands of Mr. Baldwin's men illuminated the backs of the fleeing smugglers as they ran pell-mell down the few steps above which was the trap door that formed part of the landing platform in the boathouse. Flinging the door open the men leaped out, Mr. Baldwin close at their heels, but instead of landing in the power launch as they expected, the surprised smugglers, blinded by the bright light from the Coast Guard cutter, fell sprawling into the water just as the row boat bearing Captain Erwin and his men entered the enclosure. An instant later Mr. Baldwin and his men, together with the four excited Camp Fire girls, appeared through the opening made by the raised platform and while the Coast Guard crew fished the captured smugglers out of the water, Mrs. Evans and Alice and Dolores, Mabel, Anita and Lenore shouted to each other joyously, thrilled over the capture of the men they had been sent to apprehend and happy at being re-united once again. Turning the captured smugglers over to Captain Erwin, Mr. Baldwin instructed him to turn the men over to the Customs officials in New York at once, detailing some of his men to go along as special guards and to prefer formal charges against the prisoners. As the smugglers were being pulled from the water into Captain Erwin's row boat, the two men Mr. Baldwin had sent to capture the remainder of the band of outlaws arrived on the scene with their prisoners securely handcuffed to each other. Waiting until Alice and Mrs. Evans had disembarked from their row boat into the entrance to the tunnel where they joined the others, Captain Erwin transferred the captured men to their boat in charge of Lieutenant Graham and calling a cheery farewell to the girls, ordered his men to row back to their ship with the boat load of tightly bound, erstwhile smugglers in tow.

Retracing their steps through the tunnel, Mrs. Evans and the girls told each other of each one's share in the adventure until, when they had finished, Mr. Baldwin had a complete story of the night's happenings to include in his report to his superiors in the United States Customs Service.

Arrived in the living room of the old mansion, Mr. Baldwin bid Mrs. Evans and the girls goodnight.

"Of course," he grinned, "I can't ever begin to thank you for what you have done. I want you to know, however, that if there is anything I can ever do for you, no matter what it is, please don't hesitate to call on me. And now I've got to rush back to New York and develop these pictures. You can stay here as long as you like or until you're ready to go back to Oakdale but when you do return home, let me know so I can arrange for your transportation. I'm sorry I didn't have time to send you that car I promised, by the way, but if you want to stay on here, I'll send one tomorrow."

"Thank you very much," smiled Mrs. Evans, "and as for remaining here, I'll leave that up to the girls, although we really should return to Oakdale and school right away."

"But what we should do and what we're going to do are two entirely different things!" laughed Dolores as the rest of the girls joined her in jubilant declarations of their intentions to accept Mr. Baldwin's offer and remain a while longer in the old mansion on the once beautiful Dutton estate.

Some days later a telephone call from Mr. Baldwin summoned Mrs. Evans and the girls to his office in New York where they were asked to identify the men whose capture they had been instrumental in effecting. The girls had no difficulty in picking out Manuel and Ramon, remembering them as the two men they had seen in the subway train when they were going to Long Island and now recognizing their voices as belonging to the two men who had captured Mabel and Dolores and later helped bind Mrs. Evans and Alice in the power launch. Faced by the girls, they admitted their guilt and implicated their comrades, making further identification unnecessary.

The warm spring days passed swiftly for the five Camp Fire girls and their leader while they enjoyed themselves swimming, boating and resting beneath the big shade trees. Although they were loath to admit it, they were forced to agree with Mrs. Evans one day when she told them it was time they were returning home. A few days later, their bags packed, they bid farewell to Sam Hawkins and his wife and climbing into the old, broken down auto that had carried them to the Dutton mansion, they rattled and banged away to the little Long Island town where they would take the train that would carry them into New York and the Grand Central depot and thence on another train to Oakdale and home.

PART II

Aboard Ship

CHAPTER I

The train from New York to Oakdale slid to a halt in the long, cool twilight of the railroad terminal at Cleveland, halfway between the two points, and portly Mabel Chapman looked up from the magazine she had been idly leafing through.

"What town is this?" she asked, peering through the train window at the scene of busy activity on the platform below her. "Seems to me I've been here before."

"Why, this is Cleveland," replied trim, dark-haired Anita Brooks. "We changed trains here the last time we went to New York, remember? That was two years ago."

"Two and a half," languidly replied tall, dark-eyed, graceful Dolores Rodriguez.

"Goodness! Time does fly, doesn't it?" remarked petite, blonde Alice Blake.

"It does and I wish we had," sighed vivacious, red-haired Lenore Rivers. "If we had taken a plane from New York, we'd have been in Oakdale hours ago instead of being only halfway there after fourteen hours of sitting in this stuffy box."

The five girls were seated in one of two private compartments they were occupying on the train that was carrying them from New York to Oakdale, their home. The five were Camp Fire girls, members of Wa-Wan-Da Camp Fire of Oakdale. They were returning from New York with their young and charming Camp Fire Guardian, Mrs. Florence Evans, where they had assisted Customs officials in tracking down and capturing a band of smugglers who were flooding the country with contraband merchandise. Residing in an abandoned mansion on Long Island Sound, the five girls and their leader discovered the secret tunnel through which the outlaw band operated and after some thrilling experiences, including the rescue of two of their number by a Coast Guard cutter, the five girls and Mrs. Evans succeeded in bringing about the capture and arrest of the smugglers.

Although the five Camp Fire girls and Mrs. Evans would have liked to spend the summer, which was just beginning, on the beautiful Long Island estate that had been the base of their operations as Federal Investigators and Mr. James Baldwin, the Deputy Collector of Customs who had enlisted their aid, told them they could remain as long as they wished, they knew that the completion of their work compelled them to return to Oakdale and school. Since there was no necessity for haste, the girls had left New York as they had arrived, by train, which was the reason for Lenore's lament, their active individual preferring the speedier form of air travel.

The train on which Mrs. Evans and the girls were riding was scheduled for a stopover of fifteen minutes in Cleveland while an additional string of cars was attached to it for the remainder of the journey. For a few minutes the air was filled with bumping, scraping, jarring noises as the extra cars were being coupled to the train. Suddenly Lenore leaped to her feet as a clearer, different sound made itself heard above the general din coming in through the open windows of the room.

"Someone's knocking," she announced, crossing the compartment to open the door.

Thinking that perhaps the person on the other side of the portal was the porter, Lenore stepped back in surprise when, on opening the door she saw a messenger boy standing on the threshold, holding a yellow envelope in his hand.

"Telegram for Mrs. Evans," he announced, handing the envelope to Lenore. "Sign here, please," he added, handing the surprised girl a slip of paper and a pencil.

Hastily scrawling her signature on the proffered piece of paper, Lenore gave the envelope to the Camp Fire leader while, with a sudden lurch, the train began pulling forward and stopping, preparatory to rolling out of the Cleveland station. Tearing open the envelope Mrs. Evans hastily scanned the message and then caught her breath in sharp surprise as the full import of the words printed on the yellow sheet of paper reached her brain.

"Quick, girls!" she cried, leaping from her seat, "Get your bags, we've got to get off this train at once! Don't stop to ask questions, I'll tell you all about it later. Hurry, we're not out of the station yet and if we move fast, we can make it!"

Instantly obeying their leader's commands, the five Camp Fire girls snatched their suitcases and, racing from the compartment, dashed down the short corridor to the rear of the railroad car where the porter was just about to close and lock the exit door. Without a moment's hesitation, the five girls and pretty Mrs. Evans jumped from the slowly moving train, calling to the astonished porter to throw their luggage out after them. Anita, Lenore, Alice, Dolores and Mrs. Evans managed to keep their feet after jumping from the train, but portly Mabel went rolling over and over along the far end of the station platform until she crashed into the six suitcases piled in a heap where the porter had thrown them. Half stunned, her clothes awry and her hat jammed down over one eye, Mabel sat amid the pile of luggage and looked dazedly about her while Mrs. Evans and the four girls stood some distance from her, helpless with laughter at the comic spectacle.

"I'll bet you did this on purpose!" shouted Mabel indignantly, rising slowly and painfully to her feet, "just to see if I'm fat enough to bounce! I'll fix you!"

As she began readjusting her clothing, the others ran forward to help her but thinking that they were only coming to save their luggage from her wrath, Mabel gave one of the suitcases a vicious kick, sending it sliding directly into the path of the oncoming girls and Mrs. Evans who failed to see it coming toward them.

"Take your old luggage!" shouted Mabel defiantly, "I'll get even with you later."

But Mabel had her vengeance sooner than she expected, for Dolores, who was in the lead, tripped and fell over the suitcase, the others, unable to stop, sprawling pell-mell over one another, carrying Mabel to the ground again with them. Laughing and gasping for breath, the six girls sat amid the welter of suitcases on the station platform, their clothes rumpled, their hats askew and their hair falling into their eyes.

Suddenly Mrs. Evans extricated herself from the tangled heap and jumped to her feet, plunging her hands into the pockets of her neatly tailored suit and then, picking up her purse from the ground where it had fallen, rummaged frantically through it, but what she sought was not found in either place.

"Oh dear," she wailed, "now I've gone and lost it and I don't remember the address! I'll have to wire for it, which means we'll lose a lot of valuable time."

"What did you lose?" asked Alice as she and the others scrambled to their feet.

"The telegram," replied Mrs. Evans. "I probably dropped it when we got off the train and now I suppose the wind has blown it away! I should have been more careful."

The suitcases were still scattered over the platform and as Dolores and Anita began picking them up, Lenore suddenly darted forward and snatched a bit of paper that had been concealed by one of the bags, just as it was about to blow away.

"Here it is!" she cried, handing the torn, crumpled message to her leader. "You must have dropped it when we all fell over one another. What does it say?"

"You'll find out in a minute," replied the Camp Fire leader. "Listen to this."

Smoothing out the crumpled piece of paper while the girls gathered around her Mrs. Evans read aloud the message that had caused their sudden exit from the train.

"Return to New York at once by plane," she read. "Leave train at Cleveland and report to P. R. Burton at 617 Monarch building there for instructions. (signed) James Baldwin."

"I wonder what's up, now," mused Anita as the five girls and their leader checked their bags and made their way down the long station platform to the exit gates, for James Baldwin was the Deputy Collector of Customs for the Port of New York who had enlisted their aid in apprehending the smugglers on Long Island.

Reaching the street, Mrs. Evans hailed a cab and as the girls climbed in, she gave the driver the address contained in the telegram and as the low slung, blunt-nosed, streamlined taxi shot out into the busy downtown traffic, the five girls and Mrs. Evans racked their brains to find some reason for Mr. Baldwin's sudden action.

"Maybe the smugglers escaped," suggested Dolores, "and Mr. Baldwin wants us to help capture them again but I wonder who this Mr. P. R. Burton is? I know Cleveland isn't a seaport so he can't have anything to do with Customs or smuggling."

"That's just it," replied Alice. "Cleveland *is* a seaport and has a Collector of Customs. Small freighters occasionally come in here through the Great Lakes, but if Mr. Burton is the Collector of Customs, why isn't his office in the Federal building, like all others? That telegram said his office was in the Monarch building."

"Perhaps he's just a friend of Mr. Baldwin's," suggested Anita. "Somebody he can trust with the information he wants to give us."

"That sounds reasonable enough," answered Lenore, "but if he wants us to do something else in connection with his office and if Cleveland is a seaport, why are we being sent to see somebody who is evidently not connected with the Customs Service? My theory is that this Mr. Burton wants us to help him with something."

"And that's why we're supposed to go right back to New York and Mr. Baldwin," scoffed Mabel. "The telegram plainly states that we are only to receive instructions from Mr. Burton. I think Anita has the right idea. He's just a trusted friend."

"Well, there's no use worrying about it," smiled Mrs. Evans. "We'll find out all about it when we get there, which I hope will be soon. I'm getting hungry."

"Getting?" echoed Mabel. "I've been starving for the past two hours. Let's eat."

"We'd better wait and see what Mr. Burton has to say first," suggested Alice.

"Well, if there's a restaurant in or anywhere near the Monarch building," announced Mabel, "you can listen to Mr. Burton but I'm going to feed myself."

Pulling in to the curb as Mabel finished speaking, the cab came to a halt in front of a large office building and as the girls and Mrs. Evans alighted from the machine, Mabel ran a sharp and practiced eye down the street in search of a restaurant. Failing to note one, however, the disappointed girl picked up her bag and followed the others into the building. A glance at the building directory on the wall opposite the elevators assured Mrs. Evans that they were in the right place and as the elevator whisked them up to the sixth floor on which Mr. Burton's office was located, one thought occupied six alert and active minds: what was the purpose and what would be the outcome of their visit to Mr. P. R. Burton's office? Although each girl knew that the question would be answered before another minute had elapsed, they all but ran down the long corridor from the elevator to the door of Mr. Burton's office in their eagerness to learn the full meaning of the telegram received from Mr. Baldwin a short while before. Thinking that perhaps they would learn something of the nature of Mr. Burton's business from the sign on his office door and thus be able to form some accurate deductions as to the reason for their visit there, the girls were frankly disappointed when, arriving in front of room number 617, they saw that the black lettering on the glass panel merely bore the office occupant's name.

Opening the door, the five Camp Fire girls and their leader found themselves in a large, tastefully furnished ante room. A girl seated at a desk opposite the door looked up from her typewriter and smiled as the little group entered the room.

"Good morning," she said in a low, pleasant voice. "Do you wish to see Mr. Burton?"

"Yes," replied Mrs. Evans, returning the girl's smile. "I hope he isn't busy now."

"I'm afraid he is," answered the girl. "Did you have an appointment with him?"

"No," responded the Camp Fire leader, "but I think he's expecting us. Will you tell him, please, that Mrs. Evans and the girls are here? I think he'll understand."

"He certainly will!" exclaimed the girl at the desk. "He has been expecting you. Walk right in," she concluded, pointing to a door to her left, "I'm glad you've come."

As Mrs. Evans and the girls crossed the room to the door indicated by the girl at the desk, Alice knit her brows in sudden perplexity over the office girl's final statement, wondering why she should evince joy at their arrival. Her train of thought was suddenly broken, however, by her entrance, with the others into the expensively furnished private office of the man they had jumped from a moving train to see, Mr. P. R. Burton, who rose from his desk as they entered the room.

"Mrs. Evans! Girls!" he exclaimed, holding out his hand in greeting, "I can't tell you how glad I am to see you! Come in, please. Sit down, make yourselves at home. I hope you had a pleasant journey. Has my daughter told you anything yet?"

"Your daughter?" asked Mrs. Evans in surprise. "Was she to meet us at the train?"

"Why no," replied Mr. Burton, "I daresay she should have but you see, we didn't know what train you were coming on. My nephew neglected to mention it and I was so agitated, I forgot to ask him. Dorothy should have called him back and found out."

"I'm afraid I'm getting things a little mixed up," began Mrs. Evans slowly as she sank into the nearest chair. "Before we go any further, Mr. Burton, would you mind telling me just who your daughter, Dorothy, and your nephew are? You see, all we know of this entire affair is this telegram we received from Mr. Baldwin."

"Of course, of course," exclaimed Mr. Burton hastily scanning the message Mrs. Evans handed him, "how stupid of me! I hope you will pardon my apparent oversight but, you see, I'm so disturbed over this whole affair that I hardly know what I'm doing. You see, my nephew is Mr. James Baldwin, the man who sent you this wire and Dorothy and my daughter are one and the same person. You saw her as you came in just now. She's the young lady sitting behind the desk in the other room."

Hearing Mr. Burton's explanation, the puzzled expression vanished from Alice's face and as she and the others pulled their chairs closer to Mr. Burton's desk they gave the overwrought man their undivided attention while he explained to them the reason for Mr. Baldwin's telegram and their subsequent visit to his office.

"You see," he began, "I am an importer. I have agents scattered throughout Europe and Asia who do nothing but travel over the continent looking for and purchasing rare and valuable antiques and art treasures for shipment to my clients here in the United States. For instance, if you wanted a genuine Ming shawl, let us say, and wanted to be absolutely sure that the shawl was authentic, you would come to me for, although I don't like to boast, such is the reputation I have built up in the twenty years I have been in this business. Very well, you want a Ming shawl. I write to my agent in China, telling him exactly what you want and if one exists, it is found, purchased and sent directly to you. Until very recently, things went smoothly in their accustomed groove, then suddenly I began receiving complaints. Some of the articles I sold as genuine turned out to be spurious. I went to Europe and hired the best police talent available but my agents were above reproach. There was only one conclusion to be reached and that was that somewhere along the line of transit my merchandise was being stolen and imitations were being put in its place. I appealed to my nephew, James Baldwin, for aid but his office was unable to give me any information or help but when you young ladies so cleverly captured those smugglers on Long Island, I thought my problem was solved. My nephew, however, reports that those smugglers had nothing whatever to do with the loss of my goods but he suggested that I seek your assistance in tracing these mysterious disappearances. I spoke to him over the telephone early this morning and he promised to ask you to help me. The reason he wants you to return to New York at once is because the Javanese freighter, 'Siva', will dock there late this afternoon. My Australian agent is aboard the 'Siva' with a very old and valuable headdress that once belonged to ancient Javanese royalty. Although beautiful, this headdress is very large and cumbersome, necessitating its storage in the ship's hold during the voyage. Now then, although my agent is guarding it carefully and I know the man can be trusted implicitly, if this headdress is missing or if another has been put in its place somehow between Sydney, Australia, where my agent saw it stowed aboard the ship, and New York, you, Mrs. Evans and these other young ladies are to return to Java with my agent, provided you will accept this offer. You will sail on the 'Siva', which stops at several South Pacific islands between Panama and Sydney, and endeavor to find out what became of that headdress. Of course, I hope the trip won't be necessary but if it should be, will you undertake it?

One more thing," he added as Mrs. Evans was about to reply, "and that is, if this trip to Java should not be necessary, would you consider helping me in putting a stop to this pilfering of my shipments? Dorothy wanted to handle the matter herself but I need her here too much to let her go away for so long a time. What do you say?"

But before Mrs. Evans had a chance to reply, Anita leaped to her feet, shouting.

"I say yes!" she cried excitedly as the others joined her in a confusing chorus of assent while Mrs. Evans turned to the delighted Mr. Burton with a smile.

"If I'm not mistaken," she laughed, "I believe the answer is yes and I must confess, I'm as thrilled as they are. When do we start? And incidentally, could you give us a description of this Javanese headdress so we'll know it if we see it?"

"I'm afraid not," replied Mr. Burton. "I've never seen it myself but Albert Carter, my Australian agent can describe it perfectly for you but I hope you'll be able to see it for yourselves. Now then," Mr. Burton concluded looking at his watch, "it only takes two and a half hours to go to New York by plane from here so you still have plenty of time. In the meantime, suppose you let Dorothy take you to lunch and then I'll drive you out to the airport in time to catch the plane."

At the mention of the word lunch, Mabel jumped from her chair and soon the five Camp Fire girls and their leader in the company of Mr. Burton's charming daughter, Dorothy, were seated at a table in the dining room of the business woman's club of which Dorothy Burton was a member. Throughout the meal, the excited girls were unable to discuss anything save their tentative trip to Java while Dorothy bemoaned her fate at not being able to accompany the six Camp Fire adventurers.

Mrs. Evans and the girls had taken an instant liking to Dorothy Burton as she had to them and after lunch, at Dorothy's suggestion, since there was still plenty of time at their disposal, the seven girls embarked on a shopping tour that ended with Dorothy purchasing attractive and useful gifts for her six delighted guests.

Returning to the Monarch building, the girls found Mr. Burton waiting for them in his car and they picked up their luggage and drove westward through the city to the airport.

Mrs. Evans suddenly started in her seat as she remembered something.

"Please, somebody," she begged, "remind me to send a wire to Oakdale. I'm so excited, I forgot all about sending one. They'll think we've deserted them."

"Don't you worry about that," laughed Mr. Burton. "I took care of it while you were having lunch. I telephoned my nephew in New York and told him you were on your way and then obtained your addresses in Oakdale from him and sent the wires."

CHAPTER II

Roaring over the Allegheny mountains, the big passenger plane carrying the five Camp Fire girls and Mrs. Evans kept steadily on its eastward course while Lenore, relaxing in her comfortable, leather chair, gazed out of the window and grinned.

"This is what I call travelling," she announced. "No more poking along in stuffy old trains for me. Just think, it took us thirteen hours to get to Cleveland from New York by train and it's only taking two and one half hours to cover the same distance by plane and it's every bit as comfortable and safe as a train, too."

"You ought to go to the company's office when we get to New York," giggled Anita, "and apply for a job in their advertising department. They could use you."

"What time is it?" asked Dolores. "We should be there, shouldn't we?"

"We're due to land in about forty-five minutes," replied Alice, glancing at her wrist watch, "and a half hour from then should see us in New York again."

"They ought to have landing fields on top of some of those tall buildings," suggested Mabel, "so we could land in New York proper instead of in New Jersey."

"Perhaps," smiled Mrs. Evans, "but in our case, I think landing in New Jersey will be to our advantage. We can phone Mr. Baldwin from the airport and if the 'Siva' is about to dock, we can take a ferry across the East river and be within a few blocks of the 'Siva's' pier when she comes in. We could meet Mr. Baldwin there, too."

As the big plane roared on, the girls and Mrs. Evans lapsed into silence as they watched the ever changing panorama below them. Occasionally the plane's trimly uniformed and attractive stewardess would pass through the compartment, making sure her passengers were comfortable and supplied with such reading material and refreshments as they desired but since Mrs. Evans and the girls were the only passengers aboard the plane, the pretty stewardess found her duties extremely light for the five Camp Fire girls and their leader were too excited over their new assignment to read or partake of the iced tea and other refreshments she offered.

Suddenly Alice gasped and pointed to the window next to her at the sight that met her eyes. Far below them and blanketed in a shroud of heavy, white smoke rose the tall spires of New York city, gleaming in the bright summer sun. The entire island of Manhattan was visible from the plane, surrounded by its rivers and fronted by the ocean but from the altitude of the plane, the water looked like a narrow band of bright silver girding that section of the most densely populated city in the world. The boats on the river seemed but tiny specks, trailing minute puffs of smoke while the towering peak of the Empire State building seemed no bigger than a church steeple in Oakdale. Fascinated, the girls watched with bated breath as the big plane seemed to pause momentarily in its flight and then, with a graceful swoop, descended upon and circled the vast city below them. The roar of the motors died and the plane floated swiftly over the East river, dividing the states of New York and New Jersey, and came to a smooth and perfect landing at the New Jersey airport. Attendants rushed to open the door and let down the steps of the plane and as its passengers alighted, Mabel turned their luggage over to two Red Caps while Mrs. Evans went to telephone Mr. Baldwin, announcing their arrival.

As she was about to enter the waiting room, Anita, who had been following her, with the others, at a slower pace, suddenly seized Lenore's arm and pointed to where a group of people were standing near one of the hangars that lined the field.

"There he is!" she cried. "There's Mr. Baldwin over there by that hangar! You tell him we're here while I go get Mrs. Evans. Hurry, before he thinks we haven't come and goes away. He looks worried. I'll bet there's more to this than we think."

While Lenore ran to catch up with Mrs. Evans, the other girls hastened in the direction of the hangar and a few minutes later, Mr. Baldwin, Mrs. Evans and the five Camp Fire girls were in a taxi, speeding toward the New Jersey ferryboat docks. Dismissing the cab at the entrance to the docks, the little group forced their way through the milling crowds and arrived just in time to be the last to board the broad, flat river ferry before it nosed out into the busy river traffic.

"It will take us about fifteen minutes to cross the river in this thing," Mr. Baldwin explained as he, Mrs. Evans and the girls pushed their way to the open, front end of the boat, "whereas if we had taken the Hudson Tube or driven through the Holland Tunnel, the trip would have taken only five or ten minutes at best."

"When does the 'Siva' dock?" asked Dolores, turning to Mr. Baldwin suddenly.

"In about half an hour," replied Mr. Baldwin, "that's why we took the ferry. You see," he explained, "although it will take five to ten minutes longer to get across the river this way, we'll land much nearer the 'Siva's' dock in New York."

"But the 'Siva' won't be there," answered Dolores, pointing to a newspaper in the hands of a man standing next to her, "unless you know about that article."

"What are you talking about?" asked Mr. Baldwin perplexedly, following the direction of Dolores' gaze. "What makes you say the 'Siva' isn't going to dock on schedule?"

"We'll get a newspaper as soon as we dock," replied Dolores since the man at whose paper she had been looking had turned the page containing the article she had referred to. "I don't know if you know it or not but there's an article in there that says the 'Siva' isn't going to dock today. It said so in the headline."

"Good grief!" gasped Mr. Baldwin and whirling around, he snatched the paper from the astonished man's hand and began leafing wildly through it, in search of the article Dolores had mentioned. So great was his excitement, however, that he was unable to fold the paper properly with the result that the various sections came apart in his hands and, aided by the breeze from the river, the Deputy Collector of Customs for the Port of New York found himself helplessly enveloped in clinging, smothering masses of newspaper. While Mr. Baldwin sought to disentangle himself from his fluttering shrouds, the erstwhile owner of the paper endeavored to reclaim his property so that by the time the ferry warped into its dock a few minutes later, the paper was in shreds, its owner was loudly demanding police protection and Mr. Baldwin, his necktie under one ear and his hat jammed down over his eyes, was futilely trying to silence the man's vociferations. The other passengers, highly amused at the spectacle, stood about in grinning groups while Mrs. Evans and the girls leaned against the railing, too helpless with laughter to go to the aid of the thoroughly exasperated and enraged Deputy Collector of Customs just then.

As soon as the gates in front of the boat were raised, after it docked, Mr. Baldwin dashed through the crowd, Mrs. Evans and the still laughing girls following him as best they could. Catching up with him as he stopped at a newsstand to buy a paper

Mrs. Evans and the girls peered over his shoulder as he swiftly turned to the marine news section and began scanning its columns for the article Dolores had seen.

"Here it is!" he suddenly exclaimed as his eye caught the sought for headline. "Listen to this: 'Siva' Ordered to Quarantine; Freighter unable to land until health authorities investigate report," he read. "Reports that the Sloane Line freighter 'Siva', bound to New York from Sydney, Australia, is carrying diseased Javanese feathers today caused port authorities to order the ship quarantined until a thorough investigation could be made. According to Health Officer E. R. Trent, the feathers, if diseased, will be burned before the 'Siva' will be allowed to land."

"The headdress!" gasped Alice as Mr. Baldwin finished reading the article.

"I don't see why they have to be burned, even if they are diseased," protested Mabel. "Couldn't they be fumigated or cleaned, somehow?"

"I'm afraid not," replied Mr. Baldwin shortly. "We don't know enough about these tropical diseases and infections to permit us to do anything like that."

"Well, what are we going to do?" asked Lenore. "Go back to Oakdale?"

"We'll find out about those feathers first," answered Mrs. Evans.

"We'll find out about them right now," replied Mr. Baldwin suddenly. "Wait here for me. I'm going to phone my office and get all the information I can on this thing. There's something wrong somewhere and I'm going to find out just what, where and how it is. My uncle told me over the phone that the Javanese authorities were mailing him a certificate or something attesting to the health of that headdress."

"In that case," replied Alice, "all we have to do is wait until the certificate arrives, show it to the Port health authorities and the headdress won't be burned."

"But suppose they burn it before the certificate arrives?" asked Dolores.

"They won't if Mr. Baldwin tells them not to," answered Anita, "and that's just what you're going to do, isn't it?" she finished, turning to the Deputy Collector.

"I don't know," he sighed. "If those feathers are diseased and I issue an order to delay burning them until I can get that certificate from my uncle, that will mean holding the 'Siva' in Quarantine for several days with the result that the Sloane Line and the shippers who have cargoes aboard her will lose money. Of course, if the feathers aren't diseased, everything will be all right, but in either case, it looks as though you girls have come on a wild goose chase because evidently that headdress is aboard the 'Siva' which means you won't have to go sailing half way around the world looking for it. I'm sorry to have caused you so much trouble."

"No trouble at all," called Mabel as Mr. Baldwin went to telephone his office.

"We might have to go to Java anyway," Lenore mused as she and the others waited for Mr. Baldwin's return. "That headdress, whether it's diseased or not, might not be the real thing. Remember, Mr. Burton told us that imitations had been substituted for the real thing before. I'm inclined to believe that that is what has happened to Mr. Burton's Javanese headdress. The real one was stolen and an imitation is to be burned in its place so that whoever stole the real one can sell it and be safe from prosecution since the headdress, having been legally destroyed, ceases to exist and becomes another headdress, but not the stolen one. See what I mean?"

"No," sighed Mabel wearily, "and I don't think you do either. I'm afraid too much travelling doesn't agree with you. Why don't you go to a hotel and rest until this whole thing blows over?"

Mrs. Evans, however, as soon as she heard Lenore's theory, seized her arm.

"That's it!" she cried excitedly. "That's just what has happened! Somebody aboard those other ships and now on the 'Siva' has been stealing Mr. Burton's merchandise! Until now it has been possible to duplicate the importations and keep the originals for future disposal but evidently there is only one such Javanese headdress, whereas there might have been other Ming shawls or Satsuma vases, no matter how few. With the one and only original headdress legally destroyed, despite the fact, which we will have to prove, that it is an imitation, the real article's value will be increased when it is finally brought to light and its genuineness proved by someone who knows all about such things. As Lenore said, the thieves will be safe from prosecution because ownership cannot be proved, since the head dress was allegedly and legally destroyed and the original, when produced, can be said to be another and companion piece to the one that was burned! In order to check up, however, we'll have to get a list of the names of the ships that have carried Mr. Burton's importations since they began to disappear and have Mr. Baldwin's men question the crews. We could also have one of Mr. Burton's agents make a test shipment of something that only seems to be of great value and catch the thieves that way."

"Great!" cried the others in an enthusiastic chorus when Mrs. Evans had finished.

"You should be a detective!" laughed Alice. "I'll speak to my Dad about getting you a job on the Oakdale police force when we get back. Detective Florence Evans!"

"Of course," sighed Mabel, "if things turn out as you say, I'm glad for Mr. Burton's sake but even so, if I had thought of that, I don't think I would have said anything about it. At least not just yet, anyway. I always think of the future."

"What has thinking of the future got to do with not advancing the same theory, assuming the impossible, that you had brains enough to think of it?" asked Anita.

"Because," answered Mabel disconsolately, "thanks to Mrs. Evans' swell idea, all my rosy dreams of a voyage to the mystic and enchanted isle of Java have gone blah!"

"I was thinking of the same thing," sighed Dolores. "The nearest I'll ever get to Java now, I guess, is a cup of coffee or a movie travelogue if I'm lucky."

"That reminds me," suddenly exclaimed Mabel, "when, if ever, do we eat?"

"Why you only had lunch three hours ago," protested Lenore. "You can't be hungry."

"But I am!" wailed Mabel. "You've no idea what air travel does to the appetite."

"According to that," grinned Alice, "you must have been born in an airplane."

A moment later Mr. Baldwin arrived from the drug store where he had gone to telephone his office but eager as they were to report Lenore's and Mrs. Evans' theory the girls waited until Mr. Baldwin had informed them of the results of his telephone conversation, which, as they listened, made the girls' eyes grow round with surprise.

"Great Scott!" he gasped as he joined the little group in front of the newsstand. "Never in all my life have I encountered such a thoroughly tangled mess as this situation is turning out to be! No one at my office knew anything about diseased Javanese feathers although they did know that the 'Siva' was to be sent to Quarantine before docking but no one knew why so I phoned the health officers on Quarantine island. They told me that the reason the

'Siva' was in Quarantine was because it was thought one of the crew was suffering from some tropical disease. The man was taken off the boat and put in the hospital there for the usual examination and observation and after the other members of the crew and my uncle's agent, Albert Carter, had satisfied the doctors that they were all right, the 'Siva' was allowed to proceed and will dock in about five minutes. What I can't understand, though," finished the puzzled man, "is how the story about the feathers got into the newspaper. No one except ourselves and Albert Carter knows about them and according to reports from Quarantine, they certainly are not diseased. I give up!"

"Despair not!" grinned Mabel with a melodramatic gesture. "While you were gone, the giant intellects of Wa-Wan-Da Camp Fire's brain trust have been very brainy. They have very considerately thought out a way to clear up everything in order to keep me from taking that trip to Java. They are going to keep me standing in front of this newsstand instead until I starve to death, an action I began an hour ago."

"You see," explained Alice, "Mrs. Evans and Lenore have hit upon an idea that I think will acount for the disappearance of your uncle's goods. I think it might also explain the present mix up between your office and the health officials, to say nothing of giving us a pretty good inkling of how the story about the feathers got into the newspaper. But first, I think we ought to go down to the 'Siva's' dock and see if that headdress is really aboard. Mr. Carter might be able to give us some information, too. How far is the dock from here?" she asked in conclusion.

"Just a few blocks," replied Mr. Baldwin. "We can walk the distance in less time than it would take to call a cab. But what is all this theorizing you've been up to? Evidently you already know more about this whole thing than I do. Don't be selfish. Throw a few hints and theories my way."

"We were coming to that," answered Lenore and as the little group moved away from where they had been standing in front of the newsstand, she explained to the highly elated Mr. Baldwin the theory she and Mrs. Evans had worked out a while ago.

"By Jove!" exclaimed the delighted Deputy Collector of Customs as he led the way to the 'Siva's' dock, "that seems to fit the picture like a made to order frame! Come on! Let's get aboard at once and see what Mr. Carter has to say about this."

The 'Siva', up whose gangplank Mr. Baldwin led the five Camp Fire girls and their leader, was a large, clumsy looking freighter, its sides painted a rusty black and its two tall funnels banded with alternate stripes of red and blue, the colors of the Sloane Line which owned her. Mounted on the lower deck at both ends of the boat were square, massive looking structures from which protruded derricks, used in loading and unloading cargoes while between them and mounted in tiers in the center of the ship was the superstructure containing the living quarters of the officers and a few cabins for occa-

tine island sez t'war'nt so but they took ol' Pete along anyhow."

Stopping in front of one of the doors that lined the top deck, Captain Corcoran raised his huge fist and brought it crashing down on the heavy oak panel while Mr. Baldwin, Mrs. Evans and the girls grouped themselves eagerly about him, anxious to see the Javanese headdress that was the cause of their presence aboard the 'Siva.'

As the captain's hand dropped to his side, the anxiously waiting girls expected to see the door of the cabin open in response to his knock but instead they heard a furtive, scurrying sound as though someone wearing house slippers was running across the floor. The noise ended suddenly in a loud thump which was followed by several loud and angry exclamations and a second later the door flew open, revealing Mr. Albert Carter of Sydney, Australia, clad in a bright hued dressing gown, his face covered with shaving lather, his razor still clutched in one hand while in the other he held a large, blue steel automatic pistol which wavered in his none too firm grasp.

"P-p-please d-don't try t-to c-come in," he sputtered, "or—or I sh-shall b-be f-forced to-to sh-shoot! G-go a-away, a-all of y-you, p-please. I-I r-really m-must f-finish sh-shaving. G-good d-day. I-I'm s-sorry I-I c-can't ask y-you a-all i-in."

For a moment the five Camp Fire girls and their leader were too surprised to move or speak but before Mr. Baldwin could explain their presence, Captain Corcoran threw back his massive head and roared with laughter while Mr. Carter looked at him with a pained expression.

CHAPTER III

Mr. Albert Carter of Sydney, Australia, was a small man with small, sharp features and a shining, bald head. As he spoke to the astonished group outside his door, his small, black eyes darted from one to the other of his visitors suspiciously while he held his gun ready for instant use but as soon as Captain Corcoran's hearty laugh snapped the tension, he lowered his weapon and a pained, exasperated expression crossed his face. Turning around, he tossed his gun onto the bed behind him.

"Now that you've spoiled it," he sighed, "you might as well bring them in. I do wish you had let me intimidate them, even if it had been for just a few minutes."

"Pleasant fellow," murmured Mabel to Anita as they stepped into the cabin.

"Oh, but I am!" replied Mr. Carter quickly as he overheard what Mabel said. "It's only that I've never really had a chance to use that gun since I bought it and I did so want to try it out. But it's just as well, I suppose. I'm Albert Carter," he concluded, offering his hand to Mabel who was standing nearest to him.

"How do you do?" she smiled, accepting the proffered hand. "I'm Mabel Chapman."

Introducing Mrs. Evans, the other girls and Mr. Baldwin to Mr. Carter, Mabel was about to present Captain Corcoran also, forgetting, for the moment that the two men must already know each other, when Mr. Carter backed hastily away, shaking his head.

"Oh no, not again," he protested. "I flatly refuse. I shook hands with him in Sydney and he reduced my fingers to a helpless pulp. I refuse to be made pulp of again."

"Why, I barely touched ye!" protested the captain. "Gimme yer hand an' I'll show ye whut a real handshake is like, th' kind one seaman gives another in greetin'!"

"No, thank you," politely refused Mr. Carter. "Try it on the hull of your ship."

"I quite agree with Mr. Carter, Mike," grinned Mr. Baldwin, feeling his own hand gingerly, "but tell me," he went on, turning to Mr. Carter, "have you that Javanese headdress with you? You see, I am Mr. Burton's nephew and these young ladies——"

"I know all about that," interrupted Mr. Carter. "I received a radiogram from Mr. Burton just a few hours ago, telling me all about you. I have the headdress here and I don't mind telling you I shall be jolly well glad to be rid of it. I don't think I've slept a wink during the whole voyage because of it. Every time I'd drop off, I'd wake with a start, thinking someone was in the room. That's why I bought that gun but, thank heaven, I've never had a chance to use it; I mean, shoot it off, you know."

"You're positive, then, that the headdress you have with you is the same one you purchased in Java?" asked Mrs. Evans.

"Why, of course," replied Mr. Carter. "Here, I'll show it to you. I've kept it in this little safe throughout the entire journey and I don't think I've had it out more than twice during that time. Of course," he went on as he unlocked the heavy, iron door of the little safe, "I'd look in every now and then to make sure it was still there, particularly every morning and night before I went to bed."

Swinging open the door of the safe, Mr. Carter reached in and drew forth a card board hat box bearing the name and address of an Australian hatter and Alice, whose merry, blue eyes were always on the alert, noticed the word, "waterproof," printed on the side of the box. Subconsciously, she made a mental note of the fact and then with the others, crowded around Mr. Carter as he removed the lid from the box and lifted out the headdress that had brought him half way around the world.

As the bright afternoon sun, streaming through the porthole of Mr. Carter's cabin, fell on the headdress the girls and Mrs. Evans opened their eyes wide and gasps of admiration escaped them as they beheld the savage beauty of the many colored feathers, held in place by gold and jade ornaments that comprised the headgear that had been worn by primitive Javanese priests many centuries ago.

Thrilled, the five Camp Fire girls and their leader examined the headdress while Mr. Carter explained how and of what materials it had been made. The broad band into which the brilliantly colored feathers were fitted was woven, the girls were told, from strips of dried tiger skin with the fur turned inside so that it rested against the forehead of the wearer. The outside of the headband was studded with intricately carved ornaments of gold, each one of which, Mr. Carter explained, held one or more feathers in place, according to the size of the gold piece. Between each golden ornament and above and below them, were smaller bits of jade, each carved to represent a Javanese spirit and each, Mr. Carter further told the delighted girls, having the power, supposedly, to cure anything from a stubbed toe to serious wounds inflicted in battle. The gold ornaments, he went on, were for driving the evil spirits of disease out of afflicted Javanese natives. The feathers themselves, which resembled ostrich plumes rather than the stiff, goose-like feathers the girls had somehow expected, were dyed in bright blues, reds, yellows, greens and purples and as the girls examined them, they saw that no two colors were alike. Lenore counted six different shades of yellow and Mabel pointed to three red plumes that ranged in shade from deep crimson to bright scarlet, while Alice, who was examining the headband, pointed to a jade ornament that seemed to be loose.

"One of these doo-dads back here seems to be coming off," she announced to Mr. Carter, fingering the bit of jade she had reference to. "It's hanging by a thread."

"Hair would be more correct," smiled Mr. Carter. "Those ornaments were sewn on with human hair and the Javanese consider it a great honor to have their hair used as thread for the high priest's headdress and other articles of his clothing."

"Well," announced Mr. Baldwin, finally as the girls and Mrs. Evans finished their inspection of the headdress, "everything seems to be O.K. I'm sorry I brought you girls back to New York on a wild goose chase but, of course, I had no way of knowing how matters would turn out until Mr. Carter arrived. Shall we go ashore?"

"What about the headdress?" asked Dolores. "I mean, aren't we supposed to see that it gets delivered to the proper party? And then, too, aren't we to try to find out what became of those other shipments of Mr. Burton's that were lost?"

"No," smiled Mr. Baldwin. "Thanks to the splendid brain work of Mrs. Evans and Lenore, I think my staff of investigators can clear that matter up very soon but insofar as delivering the headdress is concerned, you can assist with that if you want to, provided Mr. Carter is willing. You see, he's flying to Cleveland with it this afternoon to hand it over to my uncle. You can go with him, if you wish and return to Oakdale from there. But whatever you do, let me thank you again for your splendid co-operation, both past and present. And now, how about some lunch?"

"Hooray!" shouted Mabel. "That's music to these eager ears. Come on, let's go!"

While the others had been speaking, Alice had been examining the headdress again, her blond head bent close over the brightly colored plumes and as the others prepared to leave the cabin, Mr. Carter stepped forward to replace the headgear in its box before putting it back in the safe. Suddenly the Camp Fire girl looked up from her close scrutiny and faced Mr. Carter, a frown creasing her level brows.

"You said these ornaments were sewn on with human hair, didn't you?" she asked.

"Why yes," replied the puzzled Mr. Carter. "They are. Why do you ask?"

"Because," answered Alice in a low voice, pointing to the loose bit of jade, "if I'm not mistaken, that particular jade ornament is hanging by a piece of common, ordinary darning thread! Look for yourself and compare this thread with a hair from Anita's or Mabel's head. They have black hair. See if they look alike to you."

"Oh, what a pal you are!" wailed Mabel. "No sooner does someone mention lunch than you go spouting fancy ideas all over the place involving torture and downright starvation."

"Impossible!" cried Mr. Carter nervously as he and the others bent over to peer more closely at the slim, black line that held the piece of jade to the headband. "The Javanese from whom I obtained this headdress are a primitive race and know noth-

"We had to," teased Lenore, "otherwise Mabel would still be dying of hunger."

"It's a good thing we don't have to go to Java," smiled Alice, "because we'd have to take two ships. One to carry us and the other to carry food for Mabel."

"I think I'd better separate you now," laughed Mrs. Evans, "before Mr. Carter gets the idea that we're taking Mabel to the museum, rather than the headdress."

"Oh, she wouldn't mind being in a museum," called Lenore from the safety of one of the two cabs Mr. Baldwin had summoned. "They *stuff* their specimens there, you know."

Before Mabel could reply, however, Mrs. Evans literally shoved her into the other cab, following close behind her with Mr. Baldwin and Mr. Carter at her heels, while Anita, Lenore, Alice and Dolores had the second taxi to themselves. Driving through New York's busy streets, stops for traffic lights were frequent but the two cabs kept consistently behind each other all the way from the dock to the museum.

Arrived at the Metropolitan Museum of Art, Mr. Baldwin led the little group up the broad stone steps and into the imposing building and, although the girls would have rather wandered aimlessly from room to room gazing at and admiring the many art treasures on display, they contented themselves with hasty glances here and there as they followed Mr. Baldwin and Mr. Carter to the elevator that whisked them up to the floor on which the Curator's office was located. The Curator was a busy man and ordinarily Mr. Carter and the six members of Wa-Wan-Da Camp Fire of Oakdale would have found it hard to obtain an interview with him but Mr. Baldwin's calling card proved an instantly acceptable ticket of admission and the little party soon found themselves in the private office of the museum's executive head.

Although she showed no outward signs of nervousness, Mrs. Evans was filled with conflicting emotions as Mr. Baldwin introduced her, the girls and Mr. Carter to the kindly old man who had charge of the museum's destinies and explained the purpose of their visit and while Mr. Carter carefully untied the strings that held the lid of his hat box in place, she wondered if she had acted wisely in suggesting this visit. Her reflections were suddenly cut short, however, as Mr. Carter lifted the headdress from the box and placed it carefully on the Curator's desk. For a moment the Curator looked at it reflectively and then, putting on his spectacles, picked it up and examined it. Switching on a lamp over his desk, the Curator next produced a magnifying glass and after further scrutinizing, with the utmost care, every inch of the gaudy plumage and ornament studded headband, while the others looked on in almost breathless silence, he removed his glasses and placed the headdress down on the desk before him. Clearing his throat, he looked at Mr. Carter.

"It's very pretty," he began, "and most cleverly designed and constructed but I'm very sorry to inform you that it's a fake! Those feathers are ordinary ostrich plumes and that headband was obviously made from somebody's old fur coat. As for those supposedly gold and jade ornaments, far from being Javanese, they can be had, in practically unlimited quantities, at any five and ten cent store. If you will look at the backs of them, you will find, plainly stamped thereon, the words, 'made in U.S.A.' I'm very sorry to disappoint you, but those are the facts."

CHAPTER IV

For a moment after the Curator finished speaking, complete silence reigned in the room. Mr. Carter opened and closed his mouth several times in an effort to speak but his stupefaction was so great that his efforts came to naught while Mr. Baldwin, Anita, Lenore, Mabel and Dolores gazed at the headdress and wondered if their ears had not deceived them. Only Mrs. Evans and Alice were not surprised by what the Curator told them and as the others slowly regained their composure, a swift glance of understanding flashed between them. They had known, before the head of the museum had even seen the headdress, that it was fraudulent.

Suddenly Mr. Carter leaped from his chair, his voice high with excitement.

"It's impossible! Impossible, I tell you!" he shouted. "That's the headdress I picked up in Java, the only original and genuine Tokko-Tokko headdress in existence. I know, because I examined it carefully before I bought it and never yet, in all the years I have been in Mr. Burton's employ, have I made even one slight mistake and from the moment it came into my possession until this very minute, it has never been further away from me than it is now. Captain Corcoran can tell you that I never left my cabin once during the entire voyage. I'm positive you've erred, sir," he finished, addressing the astonished Curator. "Examine it again and you'll see."

"But my dear sir," protested the Curator, "I *did* examine it and you heard my opinion. If you do not believe me and think you can show me where I erred, please examine the headdress yourself. I do not doubt that you did, at some time or other, purchase the original Tokko-Tokko headdress, but this is not it. I have heard of your ability to ferret out apparently lost art treasures, sir, and I have read with interest your magazine articles on the subject, so do not think I hold your opinions lightly. It has been said, however, that every man is entitled to one major mistake in his lifetime and I'm afraid, Mr. Carter, that this is yours. I'm very sorry."

Without another word, the excited Australian strode to the Curator's desk and picking up the headdress and the magnifying glass, began a careful examination of the disputed object. With unbelieving eyes, he stared through the powerful lens at the gaudily colored feathers and ornament studded headband and then slowly and with trembling hands he placed the glass back on the desk and tossed the headdress into the Curator's waste basket. Crestfallen, he slumped into a chair and buried his head in his hands while Mrs. Evans and the girls looked on sympathetically.

"You were right, sir," he moaned. "That is not the same headdress I bought in Java."

Pulling himself together with an effort, Mr. Carter sat upright in his chair and looked from one to the other of those about him with a haggard, drawn expression.

"Well," he sighed with an unsuccessful attempt at a smile, "that's that, as you Americans say. I don't know how I'm ever going to explain this to Mr. Burton but I daresay it won't make any difference. I'll simply wire him my resignation and take the next boat back to Australia. Before I leave, however, I want to thank you for the kindness and courtesy extended me during my too brief stay here and——"

"Here, here!" interrupted Mrs. Evans suddenly. "What on earth are you saying?"

"He thinks he's going to resign his post with my uncle and go back to Australia but we know differently," Mr. Baldwin announced as he rose from his chair. "Come on, Carter," he finished, taking that surprised individual by the arm, "there's a great deal of work to be done and the sooner we get started, the better. Hurry."

"Why, what do you mean?" asked Mr. Carter, surprised. "What work? What can we do?"

"Plenty," answered Mrs. Evans briskly. "If we can find the man or men who stole your headdress, we will have the thieves who have been stealing the rest of Mr. Burton's importations. Come on, we're going to catch the first boat to Australia."

Thanking the genial old Curator for his trouble, Mrs. Evans and Mr. Baldwin led the still somewhat dazed Mr. Carter from the art museum. The girls, thrilled and excited over their renewed hopes of going half way around the world, followed. In his confusion, Mr. Carter still clung to the hat box in which he had carried the headdress and as they entered the taxis Mr. Baldwin hailed, Alice took it from him. Ordering the two drivers to take them to the Customs House where he had his office, Mr. Baldwin explained to the others that it would be advisable to wait until they had reached the seclusion of his private rooms before discussing plans.

"I'll get all the information about sailing schedules," he told them as they drove off, "although there aren't many steamship lines that take the Panama route to Australia. Most of the boats leave directly from San Francisco and Los Angeles."

"That's why I had to take the 'Siva' from Australia," sighed Mr. Carter. "I was unable to get a passenger ship that would take me directly to New York and I didn't want to take the chance of having the headdress stolen while changing boats at Hawaii and probably having to change trains while crossing the United States. I'm afraid, however, all my precautions were useless. I can't see what can be done now."

"We'll go into that when we reach my office," promised Mr. Baldwin. "In the meantime, I want you to try and remember every step of your trip from the time you first obtained the headdress until we met you aboard the 'Siva'. Try to remember all of the people with whom you came in contact, who they were, what they said and what they looked like. I don't know if it will do any good, but that way, you might recall someone or some incident that will put us on the right track. Think hard."

"You don't mean that you're actually going to try to recover the headdress?" asked Mr. Carter incredulously as the full import of what Mr. Baldwin and Mrs. Evans intended to do dawned upon him. "Why, that's next to impossible! Don't you realize that that headdress is extremely valuable and whoever was clever enough to steal it from under my very nose, surely won't be fool enough to try to dispose of it at once? It will be many, many years, long after we are gone, before the rare Tokko-Tokko headdress of the Javanese medicine men sees the light of day again."

"Well, there's no harm in trying," replied Mr. Baldwin, "so start thinking."

Arrived at his office at the lower end of Manhattan, Mr. Baldwin at once began consulting the list of sailings his office received daily from the various steamship lines, while Mrs. Evans, the girls and Mr. Carter were ushered into a large, well appointed room in the center of which was a long conference table and massive leather armchairs. Seating themselves at the table while the office boy switched on the lights, the five Camp Fire girls, their young and pretty leader and Mr. Carter waited for Mr. Baldwin to join them before beginning any active discussion.

They did not have long to wait for they had barely

settled themselves when Mr. Baldwin appeared and took his place at the table with them.

"The first boat out of New York and bound in the general direction of Australia," he announced, "is the 'Comanche' and she only goes as far as Panama. She doesn't leave until tomorrow morning and you'd have to wait two days in Colon for the 'Asuncion' to come up from South America to take you to Australia. The usual time from Colon to Sydney is nine days but the 'Asuncion' takes twelve. However, I have a better idea but first I'll have to phone my uncle in Cleveland to get his O.K."

"What is it?" asked Anita as Mr. Baldwin reached for the telephone near him.

"Charter the 'Siva'," he replied. "We could leave at once and go where we pleased."

"Swell," agreed Lenore, "only chartering ocean freighters, I should imagine, is a rather expensive business. You'd better call the North Pole and ask for Santa Claus first because I don't think anyone else could be as generous and rich."

"You don't know my uncle Phil," laughed Mr. Baldwin, picking up the telephone. "He might finance the whole thing himself if his client won't. Wait and see."

"I should think," answered Mr. Carter, "that if Mr. Burton's client is rich enough to purchase the headdress, which alone is worth many times what the 'Siva' cost, he certainly would consent to Mr. Baldwin's plan. But the whole thing is fantastic. It is foolish to even attempt such an undertaking now.

The headdress was evidently stolen from me before I boarded the 'Siva', which was almost two weeks ago. It will be another two weeks before we can reach Australia again, which gives the thieves a month's start on us. It's hopeless, I tell you, hopeless."

"That's what you think," grinned Mr. Baldwin as he waited for his long distance call to go through, "but we're going to find that headdress and find it quick."

"You Americans certainly have a lot of determination," replied Mr. Carter with admiration as the telephone bell rang, "and I think you're beginning to inspire me."

"That's the spirit!" congratulated Mrs. Evans as Mr. Baldwin answered the phone.

Mr. Baldwin's conversation with his uncle was brief and to the point and when he replaced the receiver on its hook, a broad grin illuminated his boyish features.

"I was right," he chuckled. "Uncle Phil will not only pay the bill but gave me a much better idea than chartering the 'Siva', which, after all, is only a slow old freighter. He just told me that the man for whom he commissioned Mr. Carter to buy the headdress was in his office when I called just now and guess who he is? None other than J. Livingston Hunt, the famous international banker and sportsman! He's going to place his yacht at our disposal and we can leave as soon as we can get out to the yacht club in Brooklyn where she's anchored! Uncle

Phil is wagering him the cost of the trip that we recover the headdress and he's never lost a bet yet!"

Barely waiting to let Mr. Baldwin finish what he had to say, the five elated Camp Fire girls burst into unrestrained cheers and shouts and began executing a series of wild war dances about the room while Mrs. Evans vainly tried to restore order and Mr. Carter cast nervous glances around the room for the nearest exit.

Finally, when the happy and excited girls were too exhausted to continue their shouts and gyrations any longer and Mr. Baldwin found he could make himself heard again, he summoned his secretary and began issuing orders and instructions that would cover any possible emergency occurring during the voyage. His first act was to subsidize the yacht as a government ship, thus assuring its immediate entry in any port in the world, and then he deputized Mrs. Evans, the girls and Mr. Carter as special government agents, making passports unnecessary and since he himself was to accompany the girls and their leader on the trip, he empowered his secretary to act in his place during his absence. With such details taken care of and out of the way, Mr. Baldwin next phoned the yacht club in Brooklyn to advise the captain of Mr. Hunt's yacht to be ready to sail at once while Mr. Carter looked on in amazement at the Deputy Collector's unbounded energy and efficient methods.

"Well," he finally announced with satisfaction, "everything's taken care of. All we have to do now is scoot over to Brooklyn, get aboard the yacht and we're off."

"Swell!" cried Lenore, jumping up from her chair. "Let's go! Java, here we come!" The five Camp Fire girls and their leader were too thrilled and excited to think or talk of anything else save the long voyage on which they were about to embark. As they rode along in the two cabs carrying them from the lower tip of New York to Gravesend Bay in Brooklyn where the yacht was anchored, Mr. Baldwin engaged Mr. Carter in deep and earnest conversation, but no matter how much Mr. Baldwin insisted or how hard he thought, Mr. Carter could think of no person or incident that could even remotely account for the disappearance of the Javanese headdress.

"It's no use!" Mr. Carter finally sighed in despair. "I've thought of everyone and everything I met or saw during the entire trip and there's not one person or thing that I could pin even the faintest suspicion of guilt upon. I've told you repeatedly that that headdress never left my sight for an instant from the first moment I bought it until that awful scene in the Curator's office. I've given up."

"You're positive, though, that you did purchase the genuine article, aren't you?" asked Mr. Baldwin. "There's no doubt in your mind now about it, is there? You *did* purchase the one and only original Tokko-Tokko headdress in Java, didn't you?"

"Yes, yes, of course," replied Mr. Carter. "I examined it most carefully before I bought it and from that moment until now, as I said, it never left my sight."

"Then how do you account for its loss?" asked Mr. Baldwin. "It didn't walk off by itself and if it never left your sight, what did become of it? Are you positive that you didn't leave it alone for even a few minutes? How did you arrive at Sydney, Australia, from Java? Were you alone?"

"I took a boat from Java to Broome, Australia," answered Mr. Carter, "across the Indian ocean and never left my stateroom once during the entire trip. From Broome I hired a motor car and drove to Coolgardie in Southwestern Australia where I took a train to Sydney and at Sydney, as you know, I boarded the 'Siva' and came to America."

"When you drove from Broome to Coolgardie," asked Mr. Baldwin, "was there anyone with you or were you alone?"

"I was alone," answered Mr. Carter. "It was very foolish of me to make the trip alone since that part of Australia is still wild and unsettled, but I didn't care to take the risk of engaging a chauffeur for fear he might learn about the headdress and make off with it. The trip took me three days but the only living things I saw were flocks of kangaroos until I arrived at Coolgardie. I left the car at the automobile agency there and immediately boarded the train for Sydney and not once, during that entire time, did the headdress ever leave my knapsack where I carried it then."

"Are you sure that the headdress you carried in

your knapsack was the same one you bought in Java?" further questioned Mr. Baldwin. "Couldn't someone on the boat from Java to Australia know about it? It could have been stolen while you slept."

"Impossible," smiled Mr. Carter. "You see, I sewed the knapsack to my pillow every night and examined the headdress at frequent intervals to make sure I still had it and when I drove from Broome to Coolgardie, I wore the knapsack even when I made camp for the night. I wore the knapsack on the train from Coolgardie to the coast and if anyone had tried to steal it during all that time, I surely would have known it. When I reached Sydney, I saw the feathers were becoming a bit rumpled from being in the knapsack so long so I went to a hat shop there and obtained the hat box you saw me take the headdress from when you came aboard the 'Siva'. I even went to the trouble of shopping around until I obtained a waterproof box in case anything should happen while we were crossing the Pacific. I heard Captain Corcoran tell you that I hadn't once set foot out of my cabin during the entire voyage so you can see for yourself that it was impossible for anyone to steal the headdress."

"But they did," replied Mr. Baldwin, "and we're going to find out who did it and how it was done, in addition to getting that headdress back. Someone, some place, has it and we're going to find it even if we have to re-trace every step of your trip from Java to New York and back again. Things don't vanish into thin air without any reason or human assistance. Some clever thief stole a march on you, that's all."

For a moment Mr. Carter was silent and as the two cabs raced across Brooklyn bridge, he gazed down at the busy river below him, apparently lost in thought.

"I should have told you this before," he suddenly began in a low voice while still looking out of the window, "but I've been trying to put it out of my mind. What you said just now about the headdress vanishing into thin air and without human assistance, however, compels me, in all fairness to yourself and those young ladies, to tell you something I had hoped would not be necessary."

"And what is that?" asked Mr. Baldwin, his interest and curiosity aroused.

"Well," began Mr. Carter, "you'll probably think me foolish and given to a childish belief in fairy tales but if you had seen what I have seen and heard what I have heard in my travels through the Dutch East Indies, you might not be so prone to laugh as I'm sure you will when I tell you that there is something to what you said. Magic and mysticism plays an important role in the lives of the Javanese natives and although Western civilization has done away with most of the old, mystic rites (which was why I was able to obtain the headdress), there still remains traces of fanaticism that flare up now and then. Buying that headdress and taking it away from Java might have been the torch that set off such an outburst which would easily account for its disappearance. Go ahead and laugh, if you want to but I know that it's perfectly possible for those natives to get that headdress back *without my knowledge of the entire proceeding!* I have seen such things done before."

"Finally!" exclaimed Mr. Baldwin enthusiastically. "Now we have something more tangible, at least, to work on! Far from laughing at you, Mr. Carter, I congratulate you on providing us with a possible clue. Our first port of call shall be Java."

"I thought we were to go directly there anyhow," replied Mr. Carter, surprised.

"I had planned differently," answered Mr. Baldwin. "Going on the assumption that the headdress was stolen from you at some point along the route you took from Java to New York, I had planned on stopping at the Marquesas islands, Tahiti and all the other South Pacific islands the 'Siva' called at on her way from Sydney to New York. What you just told me makes that unnecessary, however. We shall go right to Java."

"But why did you want to stop at all those islands?" asked Mr. Carter. "No one boarded or left the ship there. We only stopped to unload or take on cargo."

"I know," replied Mr. Baldwin, "but still, someone might have managed to sneak aboard at one island and escape with the headdress at the next port of call."

Rolling through beautiful Prospect Park in Brooklyn, the two cabs rapidly approached the once fashionable summer resort of Bensonhurst where the yacht club was situated and as the second cab, containing Mrs. Evans and the girls followed the one in which Mr. Baldwin and Mr. Carter were riding, Dolores pointed to the many bronze tablets she saw affixed to rocks and trees they passed and asked about them.

"Most of them," answered Mrs. Evans, "commemorate a battle George Washington's troops had with the British. During the Revolution, some British troops landed at Gravesend Bay, near the place we're going to now and marched up here where they engaged in battle with the American army. There used to be a tablet near where the British landed but it's been lost, stolen or destroyed. If we have time, I'll show you the place, if I can still remember where it was."

"Then you've been here before?" asked Mabel in surprise.

"I lived in Bensonhurst when I was a little girl," replied Mrs. Evans. "It was a beautiful place then but I imagine the years have taken their toll, as usual."

A few minutes later the cabs began turning down one street and then another and as the girls watched, each street seemed to be dirtier and more crowded than the last. Looking from her cab window, Mrs. Evans sighed.

"I was right," she said. "The years have taken their toll. This, girls, is Bensonhurst, or what is left of it. It's queer now, to remember that this was once the most beautiful seaside resort on the Atlantic coast!"

As Mrs. Evans finished speaking, the cabs came to a halt before a long, low, rambling building, built in the Colonial style popular when New York was occupied by the British. A sign on the wide lawn in front of the building informed the girls that they had arrived at their destination and as they alighted from the cab, a young man wearing a naval uniform stepped from the doorway of the building to meet them. Saluting smartly as Mr. Carter and Mr. Baldwin joined Mrs. Evans and the girls, he pointed to the wide expanse of blue water visible behind the clubhouse.

"Captain Regan at your service," he smiled. "The 'Corsair' is ready to sail at once."

CHAPTER V

Long and low, rolling in the gentle swell of Gravesend Bay, the 'Corsair', placed at the disposal of the girls by her owner, J. Livingston Hunt, rode at anchor with full steam up, ready to sail as soon as the excited group on shore boarded her.

Following Captain Regan along a well worn path that led from the street, past the club building and down to the beach, the girls, Mrs. Evans, Mr. Baldwin and Mr. Carter ran their eyes admiringly over the trim lines of the 'Corsair' and thrilled with anticipation over the prospect of living aboard her for an indefinite period. As the happy and excited group passed the clubhouse on their way to the beach, a uniformed servant left the building and approached them. For a moment he seemed to hesitate and then, as though suddenly making up his mind, stopped Mr. Baldwin.

"Mr. James Baldwin, sir?" he asked, touching his hand to his cap in smart salute.

"Yes," replied Mr. Baldwin, surprised that the man should know him, "what is it?"

"Telegram for you, sir," answered the servant, handing over a yellow envelope.

"Thank you," answered Mr. Baldwin, "but tell me," he went on as the servant was about to walk away, “how did you know who I was? Have you ever seen me before?”

“No, sir,” replied the servant, “I never have but I know the other gentleman is Mr. Albert Carter of Australia. I was in his employ fifteen years ago as his valet.”

“Remarkable memory,” complimented Mr. Baldwin, tearing open the envelope, “I wonder if he remembers you? Oh Carter!” he called, “come here a minute, please.”

Mr. Carter had walked on ahead with Mrs. Evans but in answer to Mr. Baldwin's summons, he returned and as Mr. Baldwin looked up from a hasty perusal of the wire he had just received, he saw a puzzled expression cross the Australian's face as he saw the servant. Then suddenly his expression changed to one of amazement as he recognized the man. Darting forward, he caught him by both arms, grinning broadly.

“Why Simmons, you old rascal!” he almost shouted. “It really is you, after all these years! What on earth are you doing here? The best detective in all England, working as a servant in America! Are you, perhaps, working on a case that requires such a disguise? Mr. Baldwin! Mrs. Evans! Girls!” he cried, “I want you to meet Donald Simmons, the one man in the world who can find that headdress if it is to be found! Hurry up, man,” he went on excitedly, “run inside and tell them you're leaving! I've got a case for you that's worthy of your talents and attention.”

"But he said he was your valet fifteen years ago," began Mr. Baldwin in surprise.

"So he was," answered Mr. Carter, "and that's how I discovered his remarkable abilities as a detective. I was a private collector then and was being victimized by a series of fiendishly clever robberies that had the police completely stumped but Simmons here not only solved the case but recovered everything that had been stolen. I urged him to go to England and become a member of Scotland Yard. He finally went and that's the last I heard of him until now. What happened to you?" he concluded, turning to the obviously embarrassed man. "Didn't you succeed?"

"Er—no," replied the servant hesitatingly. "You see, sir, after I left Australia my confidence failed me and I came to America instead and I've been here ever since."

"Of all the lunkheads!" bellowed Mr. Carter. "Well, you're coming with me now."

"I think Mr. Carter is right," began Mr. Baldwin slowly, "you had better go. I think they'll need you. I was going but this telegram changes my plans. I'll have to stay here so you go in my place. I've just been called back," he explained to the others, indicating the telegram. "A re-organization of the department makes it imperative that I remain in New York but I'll keep in touch with you by radio."

"That's too bad," chorused the girls and Mrs. Evans with obvious disappointment.

"Can't you pretend you didn't get the telegram and go anyway?" asked Mabel.

"I'm afraid not," smiled Mr. Baldwin ruefully. "Orders are orders, you know."

Quickly arranging matters with the club's steward to accept Simmons' resignation at once, Mr. Baldwin accompanied Mrs. Evans, the girls and Mr. Carter down to the beach where a small motor boat was waiting to take them out to the 'Corsair', while Simmons hastily changed clothes and packed his belongings preparatory to leaving.

Helping the girls and Mrs. Evans into the boat while Simmons and Mr. Carter followed, Captain Regan gave the signal to cast off and as the little boat chugged across the bay, the five Camp Fire girls and their leader turned to wave a last goodbye to Mr. Baldwin as he stood on the beach watching them and waving in reply.

Small and compact appearing from the shore, the girls were surprised, as they approached the 'Corsair' to see how large and seaworthy she really was. As they climbed up the companion ladder to the deck, sailors took their luggage and a white uniformed stewardess approached to show them to their staterooms which adjoined one another. As the girls entered the large and beautifully furnished rooms, they gasped with admiration at the luxury of their surroundings. Each of the three rooms at their disposal had its own private bath and each room was equipped with twin beds. Mrs. Evans and Alice occupied the center room while Dolores and Mabel took the room to the right, Lenore and Anita sharing the one on the left.

From the portholes the girls could look out on the calm, blue waters of the bay and as they unpacked their bags, Anita happened to glance through the porthole nearest her. For a moment the sight that met her eyes made no impression on her; then suddenly she remembered she was on board a ship and not in a hotel room. Running to the porthole she looked out.

"Look!" she cried, turning to the others, "we're moving! We're on our way!"

"At last!" sighed Mabel, sinking down on the bed. "Golly, what a day this has been! Jumping from moving trains, catching airplanes, chartering private yachts! Whew!"

"We only jumped from one train," corrected the practical Alice, "and rode in one airplane and Mr. Baldwin obtained only one yacht for us and this is it. To hear you talk, a person would think we were acrobats giving free public performances."

"Well," commented Lenore, "we probably gave that impression but whether we did or not," she concluded, kicking off her shoes, "I'm going to do some acrobatics right now in the bathtub. I hope they have plenty of hot water on this boat."

"I'll tell the captain to send a diver down and build a fire under the boat for you," giggled Dolores as she prepared to follow Lenore's example. "I wonder how long it will take us to get to Java?" she went on, gathering up her things before going into her own room. "It took Mr. Carter almost a month to get to New York."

"Mr. Baldwin told me that was because the 'Siva' stopped at several islands on the way," replied Mrs. Evans, "and in addition to that, it took Mr. Carter almost two weeks to go from Java to Sydney, Australia. We're not going to stop at any islands so I daresay we'll be able to make the trip in less time than he did."

"I hope so," answered Mabel, "because something tells me I'm going to be seasick."

"That *would* be a tragedy," smiled Anita. "Just think of having to go two or more days without eating! I don't think you'd survive the strain and shock, Mabel."

"You won't survive the journey," threatened Mabel, "if you don't get out of here."

"Listen girls," announced Mrs. Evans, "I want you all to hurry and take your baths and get dressed because there's something I want to tell you before dinner."

"Why can't you tell us now?" asked Dolores, poking her head in through the doorway.

"Because then we'd never be ready in time for dinner," smiled Mrs. Evans. "Hurry, now, and those of you who are taking your baths first, remember the rest of us are waiting our turn. And, another thing," she admonished as the girls were about to go to their respective rooms, "is that the officers and members of the crew of this boat are not to be interfered with, no matter how good looking they are."

"This is a fine time to mention it," grinned Lenore, "but if Captain Regan is any indication of what the rest of the officers and crew are like, I'm afraid your warning is not only ill-advised but futile, if you get what I mean."

"Well, can you imagine that!" exclaimed Mabel. "A man isn't safe on his own boat any more with you around. Here we are, not out of Gravesend Bay yet and it's still practically broad daylight, and you go planning romantic moments under a tropical moon with the handsome young captain of somebody else's yacht. Such goings on! You ought to be ashamed of yourself. I wonder what the first mate looks like?"

"You should be more interested in the cook," shouted Anita from her bathtub.

Further discussion of the officers and crew of the 'Corsair' was interrupted by the arrival of the stewardess who came to assist Mrs. Evans and the girls with their toilettes. The six members of Wa-Wan-Da Camp Fire and the elderly, good natured stewardess immediately took a liking to each other, however, and a few moments after her arrival, Mrs. Crawford, the stewardess, found herself chuckling and giggling as much as the girls themselves as she answered their questions about Captain Regan and the other officers, whom, she told the girls slyly, were all eligible bachelors who looked upon their arrival aboard the 'Corsair' as an event to be reported indignantly to J. Livingston Hunt, the yacht's wealthy owner.

"You see," she went on as she deftly twisted Dolores' long curls into an attractive coiffure, "they're not used to having women aboard the 'Corsair', and they're a little bit puzzled and frightened over what to do about you. Of course, I don't count," she added with a twinkle in her eyes, "because Timothy is my nephew."

"Who is Timothy?" asked Alice as she watched Mrs. Crawford's skillful fingers.

"Timothy," replied Mrs. Crawford, "and Captain Regan are one and the same person."

"There goes your romance, Lenore!" laughed Mabel. "What chance would a girl have with a man who brings his aunt along on a South Seas cruise? Too bad, old girl."

Lenore's retort was lost, however, in the sudden chiming of bells that reached the girls in their cabins from some place on the deck of the 'Corsair' and as they hastened to put the final touches to their toilettes, for Mrs. Crawford told them that the bells announced that the evening meal was about to be served, a light tap was heard at the door of Mrs. Evans' stateroom where the girls were to gather before going up on deck. Mrs. Evans, who had completed her preparations and was waiting for the others, opened the door to admit Mr. Carter, who stood on the threshold, resplendent in full, formal evening attire, with Simmons standing behind him.

"We've come to take you up to dinner," he announced. "Are you all ready, now?"

"We will be, in just a second," smiled Mrs. Evans. "Suppose you go ahead and we'll catch up with you on deck. By the way," she continued, lowering her voice, "I haven't had the opportunity to tell them yet and I won't be able to now until later."

"That's what I really came down for," confessed Mr. Carter. "I've already told Simmons all about it, of course. If you could get the stewardess out of here for a few minutes, I'll tell them now because I think the sooner they know, the better."

Mr. Carter either spoke too loudly or Mrs. Crawford had very keen ears for as soon as Mr. Carter finished speaking, she turned around from the closet where she had been hanging away the girls' dresses and walked to where Mrs. Evans stood.

"If what you have to say has to do with that headdress you're after," she said, "don't mind my being here because I know all about it. You see," she went on, "in addition to being Captain Regan's aunt, I am also in the employ of Mr. Burton who borrows me now and then from the steamship line I work for as private detective. I came on board only half an hour before you did but Mr. Burton phoned me from his office in Cleveland and told me all about everything, so you all may speak freely."

"In that case," replied Mr. Carter, "you had better stay. What I wanted to tell you," he went on, addressing the girls who had gathered about him in the doorway, "is what I told Mr. Baldwin earlier today. We are going among a strange and primitive people," he continued, "people whom civilization has but barely touched. All too often, their ways are dark and not easily understood by others, such as ourselves. The best explanation I can give you of that is to recall to your minds the very mysterious manner in which my headdress disappeared. I guarded it closely all during my voyage to America and never left a room without taking it with me and yet you all know that the headdress I brought to New York was not the same one I bought in Java. How or when it was stolen, I don't know, nor do I think I shall ever know, unless Simmons, here lives up to his reputation. I hope he does but what I wish to impress most particularly upon you is that once we have passed through the Panama Canal and are cruising among the many small islands that dot the South Pacific ocean, please, under no circumstances are any of you to have anything to do with the many natives that will come aboard with fruit and other things to sell. I asked Mrs. Evans to tell you this because whether you believe in such things or not, it is my firm belief that the headdress was stolen through the agency of primitive black magic!"

For a moment after Mr. Carter had finished speaking, the girls looked at each other in blank astonishment, unable to believe what they had heard. Finally Mabel, who had a healthy disregard for anything she could not see or hear, spoke.

"Black magic?" she echoed. "Why, I gave that up before I stopped playing with paper dolls! Whatever put such an idea into your head? You must be very tired."

"Of course," sighed Mr. Carter gently, "I didn't expect any of you to believe or understand me but I have lived among those people for a good many years and I know what I'm talking about. If we stay in the South Pacific long enough, you'll find out what I mean. But I just wanted to warn you about the natives," he finished, "and since the dinner bell sounded some minutes ago, I suggest we forget about the black magic of the Melanesias and go to dinner. We're keeping the captain waiting."

The girls found the trip down the Atlantic coast and life aboard the 'Corsair' uneventful but by the end of their first week at sea they had invented several amusing games with which to pass the time and had succeeded in enticing Captain Regan and his officers to join them whenever they found themselves off duty, which the observant Mrs. Crawford found to be more and more frequent as the days passed.

Passing through the Panama Canal exactly one week after steaming out of New York, the girls watched with interest as the 'Corsair' was floated through the Gatun Locks on the Atlantic side and then gradually lowered along the fifty mile stretch of the canal, past the famous Culebra Cut that had given so much trouble during the construction of the canal and then through the Pedro Miguel and Miraflores Locks which floated the 'Corsair' out into the Pacific, a procedure that took the better part of a day, since not only did the 'Corsair' have to wait her turn, along with other vessels, to be taken through the canal, but travel in an artificial channel, Captain Regan explained, was of necessity slow because so much time was consumed in waiting for the various locks to be filled and emptied, by which procedure the boat was floated through the several levels and slopes on which the canal was constructed.

Early the next morning as the girls came on deck, they found Captain Regan just descending from the bridge above them with a pair of binoculars in his hand and as he caught sight of the five Camp Fire girls, he beckoned to them, smiling.

"Come up on the bridge with me," he invited, "I want to show you something that might change your minds about going directly to Java without stopping any place."

"What is it?" asked Dolores as they followed the captain up the steel stairs, "Some of Mr. Carter's black magic or a pirate ship about to run into us?"

"Neither," laughed Captain Regan, handing Mrs. Evans his binoculars and pointing out over the sea, "but your mention of a pirate ship came pretty near the mark."

"Is that island over there what you wanted us to look at?" asked Mrs. Evans as she peered through the powerful glasses, "or am I looking in the wrong direction?"

"No," smiled the captain, "if you see an island, you're looking in the right place all right. That's Cocos Island, one of the most talked about places in the world. You see," he went on as one by one the girls took the glasses and looked at the island, "there are persistent reports to the effect that a great deal of pirate treasure is buried there although expedition after expedition have failed to find as much as a nickel's worth of loot. But just the same some old sailor bobs up every now and then with what he claims to be the one and only original map that shows the exact location of buried treasure and another expedition sets off. I wish I had a dollar for every time Cocos Island has been dug up in the search for hidden gold. I'd have quite a comfortable treasure myself. Mr. Hunt tried it once himself some years ago but all we had to show for our trouble after two weeks of digging were a splendid collection of blisters on our hands and sprained backs."

"Are we going to pass near Tahiti?" asked Lenore, handing back the binoculars. "I hope we do. I've heard so much about it, I'd like to see it. What is it like?"

"Tahiti is a very lovely little island," replied Captain Regan, "typical of all the South Seas group. You see," he laughed, "after you've seen as much of these islands as I have, you sort of get used to them and their beauty is lost on you. As for passing near it," he continued, "I'm afraid we won't. Our course is charted somewhat to the north of Tahiti but we will pass very near Tongareva which I think is even more beautiful than Tahiti. It's smaller, but it makes up for that in charm."

"I wonder if we couldn't persuade Mr. Carter to let us land for a little while?" Anita mused. "I'm sure it wouldn't do any harm and it would be nice to feel solid earth under one's feet again, even if it would be for only a few hours or so. I'm going to ask him, anyway. You tell me when we get near Tongareva, captain," she continued with a smile, "and then I'll spring it on him so suddenly, he'll say yes!"

"All right," laughed the captain, "I'll tell you and I hope it works and if it doesn't, maybe I'll be able to help you out because I know just how you feel."

"Great!" chuckled Mabel. "I hope it does work because I've always wanted to see how I'd look in one of those grass skirts I hear they wear on these islands."

"It doesn't require much imagination to tell that," giggled Dolores, "if you've ever been on a farm and seen a bale of hay with the middle hoop broken out!"

The next moment Captain Regan found himself alone on the bridge with Mrs. Evans as Dolores fled from the wrathful Mabel's revenge and the others raced after them.

"I think I *will* ask Mr. Carter to let us go ashore at Tongareva," sighed Mrs. Evans as she watched the girls race from the bridge. "If we stay aboard too long, the girls are liable to fall into a rut from which it will be hard to arouse them. A little jaunt ashore now and then would at least serve to vary the monotony."

"You're right," agreed the captain. "I know that long voyages have the same effect on sailors, no matter how hard they have to work. Staying too long in one place is no good for anyone. That's why I'm a sailor, I guess. I can't stay put. But leave it to me, I'll manage to get you ashore at Tongareva or maybe before."

In the meantime, the Dutch proprietor of the little trading post on the much discussed island of Tongareva took his pipe from his mouth and pointed skyward.

"Mark my words, Otto," he said to his son, "government report or no government report, it will happen again this year as it has happened every year, only this year it will be worse. I know, because the others for the past five years haven't been so bad. You'd better start fixing those roofs now before it's too late."

And as the 'Corsair' ploughed through the calm, blue waters of the Pacific, those aboard her were soon to discover that the old Dutch trader was right.

CHAPTER VI

As the 'Corsair' made her way southward across the Pacific, the days grew hotter and the nights became glamorous, moonlit, velvet tapestries against which the enchanted girls moved like shadowy figures in a dream. As they neared the equator, the blistering tropical sun drove the voyagers from the deck and forced them to seek the cooler havens of their staterooms where the steady throb of the engines and the soft lapping of the water against the sides of the boat soon lulled them to sleep. The practice of sleeping through the hot days and remaining awake all during the cooler nights soon became a habit with the five Camp Fire girls and Mrs. Evans with the result that during the long voyage across the broad Pacific, they rose from their beds after sundown and sleepily sought them again shortly after the blazing orb of the sun began to make the decks of the 'Corsair' uncomfortable.

Crossing the equator two weeks after leaving New York, Captain Regan explained to the interested girls the ancient custom among those who followed the sea of initiating those who had never crossed the imaginary line before into the mythical Order of Sons and Daughters of Neptune. King Neptune himself and his court comes aboard the boat just as it is crossing the line and after a brief ceremony, the surprised travellers are inducted into the order by being suddenly doused with buckets of water pulled up over the boat's side. If any of the initiates are known to be expert swimmers, the captain further explained, they are tossed overboard where a row boat waits to pick them up and after the ceremony, the Sea King and his court provide a program of entertainment for all passengers on board. Just as the captain finished his explanation, a group of shadowy figures loomed out of the darkness and a deep, melancholy sounding voice bellowed a sudden command.

"Make way for King Neptune and his court!" it called and a moment later the thrilled girls saw a white bearded figure, dressed in long, flowing robes approach them, followed by others dressed in costumes composed of gleaming scales and seaweed and although Captain Regan had just told them what was about to happen, the five Camp Fire girls and their leader were as thrilled and as excited as though they had never heard of such proceedings before. As the procession came to a halt in front of the girls, they had no difficulty in recognizing the usually silent and shy Simmons behind the long, white beard of King Neptune with Mr. Carter, who had arrayed himself in the curtains from his stateroom, standing beside him as Official Triton Bearer. The rest of the Aquatic Court was made up of members of the crew of the 'Corsair' and although the girls knew what was coming, they were too convulsed with laughter over King Neptune's oration which he gave in pig-Latin to notice the gradual approach of the rest of the court. As the Sea Monarch drew to the conclusion of his speech, there was a sudden movement on the part of the members of the court and the next moment the girls and Mrs. Evans found themselves drenched to the skin as bucket after bucket of sea water was poured over them.

As the merry shouts of laughter following the initiation died down, the members of King Neptune's court produced various musical instruments which they had hidden along that part of the deck and as they started to play, the other officers and members of the crew who had not taken part in the ceremony came forward and asked Mrs. Evans and the girls to dance. The warm tropical breezes soon dried their wet clothing and the night sped all too swiftly for the happy girls as they laughed and danced by the light of the bright, mellow, tropical moon that shone down on the festive deck of the 'Corsair'. The stars glittered brightly in the black, cloudless sky and the huge Southern Cross gleamed down on the trim little yacht as she ploughed her way steadily across the vast expanse of water. To the happy girls it was a perfect night but to the wheelsman high on the bridge above them, matters were taking on a different and altogether unpleasant complexion. Glancing hurriedly from his compass to the barometer before him, the wheelsman turned to the man who had just arrived on the bridge to relieve him from duty and shook his head warningly.

"I don't like it, Joe," he said to the other as he relinquished the wheel. "I've been sailing these seas for a good many years but I never saw the instruments act like this. I'm going to report it to the captain. Maybe there's something wrong with them. The compass shows we're two points off our course and when I put her back on again, she jumps two points back the other way and the barometer keeps sliding up and down like a monkey on a stick. We're in for something, all right."

"By the Great Horn Spoon, you're right!" ejaculated the other as he took the helm. "Ask the skipper to come up here right away but don't let the girls hear you. We don't want to scare them if there isn't anything to be scared about, but you hurry."

Standing at a respectful distance, the sailor waited until Captain Regan finished his dance with Dolores and then, when the improvised orchestra paused for a brief intermission, he stepped forward and saluted smartly, waiting to be addressed.

"What is it, Tom?" asked the captain, turning to the sailor as Dolores was claimed by the first mate for the next dance.

"Begging your pardon, sir," replied the sailor, "but you're wanted on the bridge."

"On the bridge?" repeated the captain. "Why? Is anything wrong? Who sent you?"

"Joe sent me, sir," replied the sailor, glancing uneasily at the girls who were laughing and chatting with some officers nearby. "Perhaps you'd better come at once, sir," he went on, lowering his voice. "The barometer has been acting up a bit, sir."

The orchestra resumed its playing and as the girls and Mrs. Evans whirled off in the arms of their officer companions, Captain Regan seized the opportunity to slip away unnoticed. Hastening to the bridge, a glance at the erratic compass and barometer was sufficient to cause him to turn his attention to the weather charts spread out on a table behind him but his closest scrutiny failed to reveal any predicted climatic disturbance in that part of the Pacific ocean on which the 'Corsair' was sailing. The weather was perfect. The sea was calm and the sky was clear but Captain Regan knew from long experience that tropical storms often come without even the warning his instruments were at that moment recording, simply bursting out of nowhere, wreaking its havoc on some unsuspecting ship and then subsiding as quickly and as mysteriously as it had sprung up. Such storms, he also knew, usually confined themselves to a comparatively small area of a few hundred miles so that while one ship might be tossed about at the mercy of the waves in such a storm, another might be sailing serenely along not far away, under a clear sky.

Referring to his sailing charts, Captain Regan quickly found the 'Corsair's' position at the moment to be some miles off the coast of the Marquesas Islands. Turning to the sailor who had accompanied him back to the bridge, he issued a terse command that sent the man hurrying along the decks of the 'Corsair' to the stern.

"Ask the radio operator to get the latest weather reports from the nearest weather station," he ordered. "Stand by until they are received and then report to me."

Giving his attention to his charts and instruments again, Captain Regan was surprised to notice that the compass and barometer had ceased their capricious fluctuations and their readings now compared favorably with the predictions given on the weather charts and a few minutes later when the sailor returned with the weather report, the puzzled captain scratched his head in perplexity as he read the typewritten message handed him by the sailor, which had just been received by radio.

"All clear off Marquesas," he read, "and as far west as Fiji. Low depression area over Hawaii. Clear weather should hold for next twenty-four hours or more."

With a shrug of his shoulders, Captain Regan tossed the message aside and left the bridge to rejoin the gay party on the deck below. As the strains of the lively dance music reached him, he carefully scanned the skies above him but not even the faintest wisp of a cloud was visible as far as he could see in the bright moonlit heavens. Assured by his own observations and the favorable weather report he had just received, Captain Regan dismissed the entire matter from his mind but the old Dutch trader on the island of Tongareva looked at the sky and shook his bald head.

"The young fools won't believe an old man," he rumbled into his beard, "but they shall see. It will come and when it does they will wish they had listened to me."

Hot and exhausted from dancing, the girls and Mrs. Evans finally threw themselves into the steamer chairs that had been placed farther along the deck and while the orchestra continued playing, other members of the crew and the cook, a big, burly fellow whom the girls at first took to be a stoker, served delicious refreshments prepared especially for the occasion. Everything that was served pertained to the sea and most of the viands, with the exception of the ices, came from it or was so prepared as to give that impression. Lettuce took on the appearance of sea weed and the dainty sandwiches, over which the girls marveled since they came from such huge, masculine hands, were cut in the shape of starfish and other denizens of the deep. Although there was plenty for everyone, Mabel succeeded in making such vast inroads into the supply of refreshments that the cook was obliged to return to his galley for fresh supplies twice before Mrs. Evans was able to check her activities.

"You should have caught a whale for her," giggled Lenore as the cook returned from his second trip for more refreshments. "She's got a whale of an appetite. Ouch!"

Investigation showed Lenore's sudden exclamation

felt was part of the pitching and lurching of the boat as she was battered about by the storm tossed waves but suddenly Dolores noticed that the rolling and tossing had stopped and, save for the slow, rolling motion as the 'Corsair' leaned further and further over on her side, the boat was motionless.

With a wild cry she sprang to her feet as she realized what was happening now.

"We're sinking!" she shouted and there was a note of terror in her voice. "Mrs. Evans! Girls! Where are you? Get up! Quick! We've got to get out of here We're sinking! Hurry! Hurry! Can't you hear me? Where are you? Captain Regan! Help!"

Dolores' cries roused the girls and Mrs. Evans from their coma just as shouts and the sound of rushing feet reached them from outside their staterooms and a moment later the doors to the three staterooms flew open as Captain Regan and a few of his men, armed with flashlights and crowbars, dashed in. The girls caught their breaths sharply as the light from the electric torches held by the men showed them how sharply the boat was tilting and even as they blinked their eyes in the light of the flashlights, they saw the floor slowly rise up and turn over, becoming a wall while one of the walls became the floor as the bedclothes and mattresses slithered off the beds and landed with a splash in a rapidly growing pool of water that began swirling around their feet. The 'Corsair' was going fast!

"Everybody on deck and grab a lifebelt!" shouted

the captain as his men helped Mrs. Evans and the girls up through the doors that were now above their heads. "We struck a coral reef and tore a big hole in our side. We can't stay afloat much longer! We'll have to take to the lifeboats at once. Get into the boats as soon as you get on deck. Swenson and Jones," he ordered two of the sailors, "you, Carter and that Simmons fellow get into the same boat with the ladies. We've only another left."

The storm was still raging in all its fury as the girls and Mrs. Evans reached the deck and as they donned their lifebelts before climbing into the row-boat at the doomed ship's side, the sailors had to hold them in a firm embrace lest they be washed over-board by the gigantic waves that swept over the slanting decks.

Many miles away, on the little island of Ton-gareva, the old Dutch trader stood at his window and peered into the raging storm outside as he puffed at his long pipe.

"Maybe," he mused as he watched, "they'll believe me next time. Maybe."

CHAPTER VII

The events that followed seemed like some horrible nightmare to the still dazed girls. Somehow they found themselves sitting in the lifeboat, hanging out in space swinging and swaying at the mercy of the wind and waves, each lurch of the fast sinking ship and each giant upheaval of the sea threatening to send them crashing into the side of the ill-fated 'Corsair' and from there to be flung, helpless and broken, into the raging turmoil below them. True to the tradition of the sea, Captain Regan was the last to leave the doomed ship and as he helped the last remaining members of his crew to lower the girls' lifeboat, he tossed some gleaming metal objects into Mrs. Evans' lap, shouting instructions as to their use, but the wind snatched the words from his mouth and buried them in the roaring, pounding thunder of the waves and a moment later Mrs. Evans, the girls, Mr. Carter, Simmons and the sailors were all thrown together into the bottom of the boat as the davits by which it was being lowered gave way under the terrific lashing of the elements and dropped into the ocean.

Quick work and able seamanship on the part of the two sailors kept the small boat from capsizing but Captain Regan, clutching the twisted rail of the battered ship, saw something that escaped the notice of the lifeboat's occupants. Flinging off his heavy oilskins he roared an order to the handful of sailors and jumped.

"All hands abandon ship!" he bellowed to the sailors who had remained on board.

From his vantage point above the little lifeboat, Captain Regan had seen two forms hurtle through the air when the boat struck the waves and disappear into the vast mountains of foam-capped water that threatened to engulf the frail lifeboat and the brave captain knew that no matter how expertly their training as Camp Fire girls had taught them to swim or how efficiently their lifebelts would keep them afloat, Alice and Anita were no match for the turbulent, storm tossed ocean.

Striking the water just as the sailors pulled the lifeboat away from the lost and dangerous listing ship, Captain Regan struck out in the direction he had seen the two girls go down. The shock of hitting the cold water had cleared the senses of the two Camp Fire girls and as their lifebelts brought them to the surface, they immediately began battling the towering waves in an effort to reach the lifeboat which was rapidly leaving the scene of the wreck under the strong, steady pulls of the two sailors. Lenore, however, had seen Captain Regan leap from the ship and, clutching the arm of the sailor nearest her, pointed to his flying figure just as it struck the water. Grasping a boat hook, the man was about to pull the captain from the sea when he too, saw the bobbing, helpless figures of Alice and Anita.

The raging sea made it impossible for the sailors to hold the boat still while Captain Regan swam with first Alice and then Anita in tow to its side. Again and again the heroic captain, expending every ounce of strength at his command, would force his way through the mountainous seas to the lifeboat only to be carried away an instant later by the next wave while the two sailors, Mr. Carter and Simmons struggled valiantly to bring the boat about so that the others could be hauled aboard.

Despite the buffetings of the waves, Captain Regan never once let go his firm grip on the straps of Alice's and Anita's lifebelts but the strain of guiding the hapless 'Corsair' through the storm and the daring but fruitless effort he was making to rescue the two Camp Fire girls was beginning to tell on him. With a last, final lunge, desperately fighting for breath with bursting lungs, the exhausted captain plunged at the lifeboat again while eager, willing hands stretched out to snatch the three struggling swimmers from the sea. A brief lull in the fury of the wind enabled the sailors to hold the boat still for a moment and Mrs. Evans snatched a boat hook, ready to use it as soon as Captain Regan and the two girls came within reaching distance. Tired and weak, the captain was breathing a silent prayer of thanks for the sudden, momentary abatement of the storm as he reached for the hook Mrs. Evans held out when the tempest sprang alive again with fresh fury and the boat leaped away like a frightened thing; but Anita had felt the captain's grip on her lifebelt weaken and, shouting a word to Alice, both girls leaped through the water, hands outstretched to grasp the life saving boat hook. Their hearts sank as their hands closed on empty air instead of the firm, steel handle of the hook but a second later they shouted for joy as they felt themselves being pulled through the towering waves to the lifeboat. Alice's sleeve had caught on the long, steel hook and feeling the sudden weight, Mrs. Evans had shouted to the others for aid.

As the rest of the girls, Mr. Carter and Simmons helped Mrs. Evans haul her precious burden to the boat, Alice and Anita, realizing the gallant captain's strength was spent, held him afloat, each passing an arm around his waist while with the other they kept a firm, desperate hold on the shaft of the boat hook. A few seconds later the three lay exhausted in the bottom of the boat while the two sailors, Mr. Carter and Simmons bent all their strength to rowing away from the wreck of the 'Corsair' before the tumultuous waves sent them crashing into its now vertical side. The storm showed no signs of abating and as Captain Regan slowly regained his strength he struggled to a sitting position and reached out for the objects he had tossed to Mrs. Evans just before the lifeboat fell from its moorings on the 'Corsair'.

"Where are those things I tossed you a while ago?" he gasped. "I hope you didn't lose them. There was a rocket gun and some flares besides a compass. With the rockets kept in this lifeboat and those I saved, we ought to be able to keep on sending signals up until dawn and if we haven't been blown too far off our course, somebody will see them and we'll be picked up before daylight. If the storm dies down by daylight, I'll be able to tell our position with the aid of the sun and the compass. The Pacific is dotted with small islands and we ought to be able to strike one of them between now and daylight if we're not picked up before then."

Taking the rockets and gun Mrs. Evans handed him, Captain Regan shot a flare high into the storm darkened sky and as it burst, releasing a flood of white brilliance, the survivors caught a last glimpse of the torn hull of the 'Corsair' as she sank beneath the waves; but straining their eyes, looking in all directions, they could not see the other lifeboat. As the bright light fell hissing into the sea, the night became even darker by contrast but a second later the captain sent up another and still another flare, timing his shots so that by the time one rocket fell into the sea, another was screaming on its way skyward, bursting into a brilliant, silent appeal for help that any steamer within a fifty mile radius could not fail to see.

The storm raged in all its relentless fury throughout the night and despite the most heroic efforts on the part of the weary men at the oars, the wind and waves tossed the little lifeboat about on the open sea as though it were a bit of rag while the girls and Mrs. Evans, cold, wet and weary, huddled together in the center of the boat for the small warmth their bodies would give to one another. With aching limbs and tired eyes, they clung to each other and tried to pierce the stormy blackness of the night in a vain effort to discern the lights of some steamship that might have seen the rockets Captain Regan was still sending up at intervals. But the wind continued to howl and the waves rose to mountainous heights while the rain came pouring down in never ending torrents and only the black, storm swept night, dispelled occasionally by the flare of a rocket from Captain Regan's gun, met their gaze. Aimlessly adrift on the open, storm tossed sea, the survivors of the 'Corsair' could do nothing but wait for the storm to die down and silently pray for rescue. Knowing it was futile to waste the strength of the men any longer in trying to battle the raging sea, Captain Regan ordered them to pull in their oars and obtain a much needed rest since, despite their best efforts, the lifeboat was completely at the mercy of the wind and waves, plunging and tossing haphazardly about.

Suddenly the wind increased in force. Its howling rose to an ear splitting shriek and to the terrified girls in the frail little lifeboat it seemed that the Pacific was rising up to engulf them while the rain pelted down harder and faster than ever.

Then, as abruptly as it had started, the storm ceased. The wind died down to a balmy breeze, the rain stopped and the waves became gentle billows and in a few minutes every last vestige of a cloud had vanished from the sky. The stars twinkled brightly overhead and the large, tropical moon shone down on a quiet sea, empty save for the small lifeboat adrift on its broad, calm surface. All was peace and quiet where a moment before had raged the sound and fury of the angry elements.

Surprised at the sudden cessation of the storm, the girls looked around them and while Captain Regan, Mr. Carter, Simmons and the two sailors sprang to the oars, Mrs. Evans took the rocket pistol and while the girls handed her the flares, she fired them off into the star-studded sky and by their light Captain Regan was able to read his compass. Remembering the longitude and latitude of the 'Corsair' when it struck the reef that sent it to its doom, the captain was able to calculate, with the aid of the stars, the present position of the lifeboat and the direction and approximate distance it had drifted, but when he finished his figuring, he sighed.

"As near as I can figure out," he announced, "we've drifted and been blown over one hundred miles from where the 'Corsair' sank which means we're off the paths of the regular steamship routes. This part of the Pacific is covered with small islands, however, and, according to my figures, if we head in a southwesterly direction we should sight one of them before dawn. When the sun comes up, I'll be able to get our position more accurately with my sextant but until then, all we can do is row." Then he added sadly, "I hope the other lifeboat has met with better luck."

The warm winds soon dried the clothing of the

survivors and as the moon grew pale and the stars disappeared from the sky, the weary girls, exhausted by their battle with the elements, dropped off to sleep, each using the other as a pillow and since the approach of dawn rendered the rockets useless, Mrs. Evans, too, succumbed to the aching weariness that racked her body and slumped to the bottom of the boat, her tousled head pillowed on Captain Regan's folded uniform coat and her arms flung protectingly about the waists and shoulders of the sleeping girls around her.

On and on the little lifeboat ploughed through the Pacific ocean, two or three of the men rowing while the others rested. The coral pink of the early dawn rapidly gave way to a ruddy, fiery glow as the blazing tropical sun climbed over the horizon and began to send its scorching shafts down on the defenseless group of survivors in the open boat. In a few minutes the coolness of the dawn was changed to a baking hot inferno in which it was impossible to sleep without protection from the sun. Wearily and reluctantly the girls and Mrs. Evans opened their eyes and stretched their cramped limbs. Tired, hungry and thirsty, they sat up and blinked at the sun.

Snatching up his sextant, Captain Regan pointed it at the blazing orb, squinting through the instrument as though it were a telescope while he turned various small screws at its side and then referred to his compass on the seat beside him. Then, with a hairpin borrowed from Mrs. Evans, he scratched some figures on the wooden board that served as a seat and then announced his findings to the others.

"Our position," he told them, "is one hundred and fifty-two degrees east latitude and five degrees south longitude which means that we are practically nowhere. The Samoan Islands are the nearest inhabited place I know of and they're more than four thousand miles away but, as I said before, the Pacific is covered with small islands and if we keep on rowing, we're bound to strike one of them sooner or later. They're our only hope," he continued slowly, "because we're off the beaten path of the regular ocean liners. Our only other chance, which is even too slim to figure on, is a tramp steamer, blown off her course by the storm or a private yacht nearby."

As the day wore on, the sun's heat increased in intensity and although there was an emergency supply of food and water stored in the lifeboat, Captain Regan was loath to break into it as yet for once that was gone the little group faced death by starvation and thirst and so, despite the fact that their throats became dry and constricted and their stomachs clamored for food, the brave Camp Fire girls and their courageous leader forbore from asking for food or drink until Captain Regan, unable to withstand the suffering written so plainly on their faces, broke open the casks of water and dried bully beef and carefully rationed them out.

Feeling somewhat refreshed after they had eaten, however sparingly, the girls and Mrs. Evans took up their vigil again. Eagerly, ceaselessly six pairs of eyes scanned the blue horizon for the faintest vestige of a sail or the tiniest smudge of smoke but not so much as a torn fragment of a cloud did they see. Only the fierce, hot sun in a vast expanse of blue burned down on them and only the endless, empty sea stretched away before them. They were the only living things afloat on the broad, blue surface of the Pacific as far as their eyes could reach and farther. The heat was becoming unbearable despite the breezes that sprang from the Southern Equatorial Current and Captain Regan was preparing to rig up a protecting canopy made from the shirts and coats of the other men and his own, supported by a pair of spare oars, when Lenore suddenly sat bolt upright and an instant later grabbed the captain's binoculars from Mrs. Evans' grasp. Swiftly, anxiously she searched the heavens and then, as she saw what she had hoped she would see, a happy, joyous shout escaped her dry lips. Pointing upward, she called the attention of the others to what she saw.

"Look! Look!" she fairly screamed in her excitement. "An airplane! We're saved!"

She had heard the faint hum of the motors as the plane flew high over the ocean and, with the aid of the powerful marine binoculars, was able to see it clearly, but as soon as Captain Regan heard her shout he swiftly bound the sleeves of his shirt to an oar and began waving it frantically over his head while he instructed the other men to follow his example. Eagerly, all eyes watched the plane as it soared overhead, a tiny speck in the otherwise vast and empty sky; but despite their frantic waving and concerted shouting, the plane proceeded on its course, apparently totally unaware of the agitated group below, bobbing about on the waves. As the plane passed above them without giving any indication that the pilot had seen their signals, Captain Regan snatched up the rocket gun and three rockets. Hastily splitting them open, he swiftly manipulated the three flares into one and jammed them into the gun.

"Grab my legs, men!" he commanded as he pointed the gun upward. "There's enough powder in this gun now to throw me overboard and capsize the boat as well! Ready?"

As the two sailors held his legs and Mr. Carter and Simmons grasped him by the waist, Captain Regan took careful aim and fired. A deafening explosion and a heavy pall of black smoke followed while the little boat rocked and tossed dangerously. Without waiting to see what effect the signals had, the captain repeated the performance and as the smoke drifted away, the girls shouted with joy as they saw the plane describe a wide curve in its flight and swoop down toward them.

A moment later the roar of the plane's motors died as the big monoplane skimmed the surface of the water and then settled down as gracefully as a bird. Rowing to where the plane rested on the water, Captain Regan shouted to its occupant who was just hoisting himself out of the cockpit. Pushing back his goggles and removing his leather flying helmet, the pilot gazed in frank and open astonishment at the girls.

"For the love of Mike!" he exclaimed, climbing out on the wings. "It's you again! Am I supposed to spend the rest of my life rescuing you girls? What's up now?"

With a wild shout Mabel and Dolores returned the pilot's recognition of them.

"He's the pilot that flew us from the 'Ambassador' back to Long Island when we caught those smugglers!" Dolores gleefully explained to Mrs. Evans. "Remember?"

"That's me, all right!" grinned the pilot. "What can I do for you this time? I'm only making a solo flight across the Pacific but there's plenty of time for that!"

"We thought we were going to have to row across it until you came along," replied Mabel. "How far is it to the nearest piece of real estate and edible food?"

CHAPTER VIII

After the first few happy words of reunion, Captain Regan swiftly explained the plight of the little group of survivors while the pilot scratched his head in bewilderment. His plane would accommodate only one other person beside himself and there were eleven people in the lifeboat. The nearest island was several hundred miles away and while it would only take him a few hours to transport the shipwrecked group, one by one, from the boat to the small island, his gasoline supply would be greatly diminished by the repeated trips so that by the time only two or three remained to be taken from the boat, his gas tanks would be empty. As he explained matters to Captain Regan, Lenore spied something in the stern of the boat that she had not noticed before and instantly her alert mind solved the problem. Calling to the captain and the pilot, she pointed to the coil of strong rope lying in the bottom of the boat, half concealed by the seats.

"There's some rope," she suggested, "couldn't we be towed by the plane to land?"

"By George, that's right!" exclaimed the captain. "How about it?" he asked, turning to the aviator. "Think it'll work? There's enough rope there to let us ride at a safe distance behind you so we won't be capsized by your back wash but the chief question is, can your plane stand the strain? I'd hate to have you crack up on our account because if that won't work, you could land at the nearest island and have a rescue party sent out after us, or drop a note to the first steamer you passed."

"I guess my ship can stand it," mused the pilot slowly, measuring the lifeboat with his eyes and mentally calculating the total weight of its occupants. "I'll cut her down to half speed and take one of your men in the plane to give her more ballast. Toss me the rope and make your end fast to the bow of your boat and if anything goes wrong, drop one of those rockets in front of me as a signal. Ready?"

Quickly tying one end of the long rope to the nose of the lifeboat and the other end to the tail of the seaplane, one of the sailors settled himself in the cockpit behind the pilot and as Captain Regan waved his arm as a signal to start, he tapped the pilot on the shoulder and a moment later the roar of the plane's motors split the calm silence as the plane skimmed slowly over the water and an instant later the occupants of the lifeboat were thrown together in a confused heap as the rope became taut and the little boat leaped forward in the wake of the seaplane. With his eyes never wavering from the rope, Captain Regan held the loaded rocket gun in his hand ready for immediate use but the rope held and as the lifeboat went skimming swiftly over the waves, the girls and Mrs. Evans eagerly scanned the horizon for the welcome sight of land while Mr. Carter, Simmons and the sailor dropped off to sleep.

Suddenly Alice uttered a jubilant shout as faint and barely discernible in the distance the unmistakable outline of waving palm trees became visible. Snatching up the binoculars, Dolores looked in the direction Alice pointed and as the glasses passed from hand to hand, the outline of the island they were approaching became more clearly visible to the naked eye until the binoculars were no longer needed.

"At least it's inhabited," cried Mabel as she noticed the small group of huts clustered near the beach. "Where there's houses there are people and where there are people, there's food and where there's food, that's the place for little Mabel."

As the plane towed the lifeboat through the surf off the little island, the sailor jumped from the cockpit and cast off the rope, allowing the boat to beach itself. He taxied his plane as close to the shore as he could get. Six pairs of arms were beckoning him landward, but he shouted, "This stopping off place is not on my itinerary, so I'm going on, but I'll send a message to the states announcing your safety. Goodbye."

A chorus of "Thanks," and "Goodbye" was drowned by the sudden noise of the racing motor and as the eager, happy girls leaped into the water and waded to the shore, they turned to wave farewell to the pilot who had rescued them as he raced over the water and then soared up and away on his interrupted flight across the Pacific.

A crowd of curious, chattering natives had gathered on the beach and as the girls emerged from the surf they saw a tall, white bearded old man push his way through the crowd and walk down the broad strip of gleaming sand toward them.

"I am Johannes Van Ryn," he announced, extending his hand. "Welcome to Tongareva."

"Tongareva?" echoed Captain Regan, grinning despite his aching weariness. "By Jove, Mrs. Evans!" he exclaimed turning to the surprised Camp Fire leader, "I said I'd get you ashore at Tongareva and I did! I'm Captain Regan," he went on, turning again to the old man, introducing Mrs. Evans, the girls, Mr. Carter and the others, "we were shipwrecked during the storm last night. I don't suppose there's such a thing as a hotel on the island, is there? And what about steamers, do they touch here often?"

"Ah, the storm!" sighed Van Ryn. "I warned the weather station about it, but they wouldn't listen to me. I knew it was coming, even if their fancy instruments told them differently. We have no hotel," he went on, answering the captain's questions, "but I guess I can put you all up at my compound and as for steamers, all we get here is an occasional tramp. The last one left two months ago but when another will come, is more than I can say. In the meantime, the island is yours. I have a small trading post here and I think I can find enough clean, whole clothing for you all."

Following the old trader from the beach to the largest of the group of huts while the curious natives trailed along behind, the weary survivors eagerly and gratefully partook of the repast consisting of fried bananas and fish Van Ryn ordered his native servants to prepare and then, utterly worn out from their unusual and hazardous experience, they fell asleep where they were, in the large, bamboo walled room in back of old Van Ryn's trading post on Tongareva Island.

While they slept, the old Dutch trader summoned a group of natives and sent them into the jungle surrounding the little village with instructions to return with enough bamboo and long grass and vines for two large huts and before nightfall the two huts were ready for occupancy. The walls and roof, like the other huts in the village, were made of bamboo poles, across which was woven the long jungle grass and vines while the floor, which rested on blocks of wood, keeping it off the ground, was made of strong, closely woven rattan. Soft, thick mats, made of woven twigs and grass served as beds and the windows were merely openings in the walls covered by filmy mosquito netting. Other than the beds, the new huts were devoid of furniture for the kindly old Dutch trader meant to have the survivors as his mealtime guests as long as they remained on the island, for visitors were a rare treat to him.

The sun completed its journey across the heavens and was well on its way to a second time around before the shipwrecked group awoke to gaze wonderingly at their new surroundings. As the memory of preceding events flashed through their minds, the girls sprang up and raced out of doors to enjoy the thrill of being on dry land once more, but as the days passed in peaceful tranquillity, they began to watch the horizon more and more anxiously in search of a ship for they realized that each day spent on Tongareva, no matter how delightful, lessened their chances by so much of ever finding the lost Javanese headdress they had come so far to recover; but the vigil remained unrewarded and as the weeks passed the five Camp Fire girls and their leader gave up all hope of ever being able to fulfil their mission since more than three months had elapsed since Mr. Carter had arrived in New York and in that time they knew that, as Mr. Carter had told them before, all trace of the missing headdress would have vanished completely, making its recovery impossible.

Mrs. Evans and the girls soon became friendly with the amiable, childlike natives and one day as they returned from a short walk through the edge of the cool jungle, S'fu, one of the native girls, approached them shyly and beckoned them to follow her. Eager for any fresh diversion, the girls and Mrs. Evans quickly accepted the invitation and as they walked along beside the dark skinned girl, she began to giggle and simper. Wondering what could cause her such embarrassment, the five Camp Fire girls and Mrs. Evans followed her into her hut where, with a quick motion, S'fu threw back an old sarong that was covering something on the floor, pointed to what lay beneath it, giggled and then dashed from the hut, leaving the puzzled girls to examine what lay at their feet. The interior of the hut was gloomy but one quick glance at the objects on the floor was sufficient for keen eyed Alice. With a cry she sprang forward and snatched them up and then raced from the hut in order to examine them more closely in the bright light of day, the others following her.

"Look!" she cried as Mrs. Evans and the others gathered around her outside the hut, "Javanese headdresses, six of them, just like the one Mr. Carter had! S'fu made these for us, evidently and I'll bet a cookie she made the other one! Let's ask her."

"I have already taken that liberty," said a voice behind them and as they looked around, the girls saw Simmons standing a few feet away from them. "I happened to see S'fu complete the manufacture of those articles," he went on, "and both Mr. Carter and myself, with the aid of Mr. Van Ryn as interpreter, questioned the girl closely with particular reference to the original but all we could obtain from her, besides a good deal of simpering, was the repeated statement that she was making them for you because she admired all of you so much and knew of no other way to express her esteem and admiration. I am convinced that the girl knows nothing of the original. The fact that these headdresses so closely resemble the one Mr. Carter so unfortunately lost is explained, according to Mr. Van Ryn, by the close connection the natives on these islands have with one another and the subsequent interlocking of their habits, customs and forms of worship. In other words, a certain rite or ceremony performed by the natives of Java will be found to have its near counterpart on an island such as this, many miles away and so on, because as these natives travelled from island to island, groups from the same starting point would settle on different islands, keeping with them the habits and customs learned in the homeland. Mr. Van Ryn has an excellent book on the subject I wish I could read. Unfortunately, it is printed in Dutch so I had to accept his translation of it."

"Would that book," asked Alice shrewdly, "account for the fact that the decorations on these headdresses, as well as the one Mr. Carter had, were made in the United States? Did you notice the words to that effect stamped on the backs of these supposedly gold ornaments? What you say about the similarity of customs among the natives might be true, but where did S'fu get her American made materials from?"

"Maybe she got them from Mr. Van Ryn's supplies at his trading post," suggested Dolores. "He showed me around the other day and you'd be surprised to see how complete his stock is. He's got everything you could think of."

"I wish he had a chocolate soda or two," sighed Mabel wistfully. "I could use that."

"Mr. Carter noticed those stampings on the backs of the ornaments," replied the Australian's former valet. "In fact that was the first thing he looked for but Mr. Van Ryn does not number such things among his supplies. We finally obtained a confession, however, from S'fu that they were given to her by a sailor from one of the ships that stopped here a few months ago. He probably traded them for some native curio."

"Well, I wish that ship or any other one would hurry up and come back so we can get away from here," sighed Lenore. "I used to think that living on a South Pacific isle, with nothing to do all day long, would be ideal but this idleness is driving me crazy. I'd even be willing to go to school all year around, just to do something."

"That gives me an idea," answered Mrs. Evans as she and the girls walked away from the hut. "Suppose we start a Camp Fire group here on Tongareva and let the girls we instruct go to the other nearby islands and start other Camp Fire units?"

The Camp Fire Guardian's suggestion met with instant approval and the following days became busy ones for the five Camp Fire girls and their leader as they initiated the delightful native girls in the arts and crafts of Camp Fire, but the American girls found they had much to learn from their island cousins concerning nature study, wood lore and the fascinating occupation of making sarongs or native dresses from the thin barks of certain trees and dyeing them in a riot of bright colors obtained from various roots and plants that grew in abundance on Tongareva.

One day while Mrs. Evans and the girls were teaching the new Camp Fire group one of the many fire lighting ceremonies, a native boy came running and shouting from the beach. Instantly the entire village dropped whatever they were doing and ran to the water's edge while the native Camp Fire girls sprang up excitedly from the circle in which they had been sitting and, grasping Mrs. Evans and the surprised girls by their hands, began pulling them toward the beach, chattering excitedly.

During the course of their stay on the island, Mrs. Evans and the girls had learned to partially understand the simple native tongue and so they understood the reason for the natives' excitement. A ship had been sighted by the boy and as they eagerly joined the crowd on the beach, Captain Regan called to them from the top of a tall tree to which he had climbed in order to get a better view of the vessel through his binoculars as it steamed slowly toward the little island's small harbor.

"It's the 'Siva'!" he shouted. "The same boat that was here about two months before we came! Get your things ready because she won't stay here long!"

CHAPTER IX

"The 'Siva'!" exclaimed Mr. Carter as he arrived on the beach in time to hear Captain Regan's announcement. "What a queer coincidence! That's the same boat that I took from Australia to the United States! I wonder if she's going back home?"

Suddenly Dolores clutched Mrs. Evans' arm convulsively as an idea struck her. Swiftly beckoning to the others, she led them apart from the chattering swarm of natives and in a voice filled with suppressed excitement, told them what had just occurred to her and as she spoke, the girls and Mrs. Evans gasped in surprise.

"We've all been fools," the tall Camp Fire girl began. "If we hadn't been so anxious to go on this trip to Java, we would never have been shipwrecked."

"An extremely sage observation," giggled Mabel, "showing you might have a brain."

"What I mean is," continued Dolores, "if we had used our heads and remained in New York, we would have had the headdress long before now to say nothing of being back in Oakdale at this very minute instead of on this island. In other words, in our excitement, we overlooked the one and only clue as to what could have happened to that headdress! Mr.

Carter was sure he never left it out of his sight for a moment and blames its disappearance on black magic, but we've been on Tongareva a long time now and none of us has seen anything like that and I daresay the natives on the other islands are pretty much like the ones here, so the black magic theory is out. What I'm trying to bring out, is that Mr. Carter's headdress was stolen while he slept and those headdresses S'fu made for us leads me to believe that the theft took place while the 'Siva' was unloading some supplies for Mr. Van Ryn here. She said a sailor gave her those brass ornaments she used, which are the same as those used on Mr. Carter's headdress, so the sailor was evidently from the 'Siva'! The man is still probably working on the boat but he must have disposed of the headdress in New York or even before he got there, at some island port."

"No, he didn't!" suddenly shouted Alice. "I know now what became of it! You were right, Dolores, we've been blind fools! We've got to get aboard the 'Siva' as soon as she drops anchor! Remember that newspaper article that said the feathers were diseased but instead of confiscating the headdress, the health authorities took a sailor from the 'Siva' into Quarantine at his own request? I'll bet a sarong that that's the man who stole the headdress! He took that method of avoiding search or suspicion in case Mr. Carter discovered the substitution before the ship docked and when he was released from Quarantine, he went back aboard the 'Siva' and stayed there until she sailed again. He didn't try to sell the headdress in New York because he was afraid that when Mr. Carter did find out about the substitution, the story would be printed in the newspapers and he'd be caught. He probably still has it with him, waiting until enough time has elapsed to bring it to light again or else he'll try to get rid of it in Australia, but in any event, we've got to get aboard the 'Siva' at once. Don't say anything to Mr. Carter, however, because if that sailor sees him, he'll probably try to destroy the headdress to avoid arrest."

Taking Captain Regan into their confidence, the girls explained their plan and obtained his promise of help. Ordering the two sailors to row Mrs. Evans and the girls out to the 'Siva' at once, Captain Regan took Mr. Carter back to their hut on the pretext that he needed his assistance in bandaging his ankle which he said he twisted slightly in climbing down out of his tree and as the two men left the beach, Mrs. Evans and the girls stepped into the lifeboat which was still on the beach and were soon on their way out to where the 'Siva' was just dropping anchor.

Bluff old Captain Corcoran greeted them with surprise and delight, explaining that he was aware of their presence on the Island. He had been notified by the government that a message of their rescue was received and since it was one of the 'Siva's' ports of call, they were to pick up the shipwrecked girls and other members of the party.

Mrs. Evans explained their mission, he smiled and winked knowingly in approval.

"That Pete Higgins is a bad 'un," he told them. "I've no doubt ye'll find whut ye're lookin' fer in his duffle. Tell ye whut I'll do. I'll put him on duty aft an' then we'll go down t' th' fo'c's'le an' take a peep through his belongin's. If ye find whut ye're after, I'll throw th' thief in irons an' then Mr. Carter kin prefer charges agan' him fur piracy on th' high seas at our next port."

Dolores and Alice had been right. Secreted in a wooden box at the bottom of the sailor's trunk, Captain Corcoran found the missing headdress as well as a handful of the cheap brass ornaments used on the imitations. A quick examination showed that the ornaments on the headdress in the sailor's trunk bore no markings on their backs as the others did and as the captain went to take Higgins into custody, the elated girls hastened back to the island to inform Mr. Carter of their discovery.

With quick, nervous fingers the excited Australian examined every inch of the headdress until the last vague doubt had vanished from his mind. Happy and almost on the verge of tears, so great was his emotion, he confirmed the authenticity of the headdress, and as he carefully packed it away in a strong box Mr. Van Ryn gave him, he thanked the girls over and over for their efforts in recovering it for him.

"Don't thank us," grinned Mabel. "If it weren't for Simmons, we would never have known about the sailor who gave S'fu those brass ornaments. Thank him."

"What I can't understand, though," mused Mr. Carter some minutes later as he, Simmons, Captain Regan, the two sailors, Mrs. Evans and the girls were being rowed out to the 'Siva', "is how Higgins managed to open the safe in which I kept the headdress and then, too, there's another thing I'd like to know and that is how he knew that this headdress was so valuable? I wonder if he'd tell me if I asked him? I think I'll try."

"Perhaps I could obtain the information you desire, sir," answered Simmons.

"That's a good idea," agreed Mr. Carter. "You seem to know how to handle people like Higgins. Go ahead but please, Simmons, stop calling me 'sir'. You're no longer my valet. You're my business partner now, in case you didn't know it. A man with your abilities and talents could find the Lost Chord if anyone wanted it and the finding of lost things is what my business depends on. It's Carter and Simmons now."

"Oh thank you, sir!" gasped the surprised Simmons, his face bright with elation.

"One more 'sir' out of you and I'll dump you overboard," warned Mr. Carter as the happy group climbed aboard the 'Siva' and were greeted by Captain Corcoran.

As the 'Siva' slowly steamed away, the girls and Mrs. Evans stood on the deck and waved a last farewell to the little island of Tongareva and their new comrades in Camp Fire who stood on the beach singing the Camp Fire girls' farewell song to their American friends whose visit they long would remember as a great event.

Later that evening as Mrs. Evans, the girls, Captain Regan and Mr. Carter were strolling around the deck, Simmons joined them and as they continued their walk he told them how Higgins knew of the value of the headdress and how he opened the safe, for no one knew the combination to it save Mr. Carter alone and he insisted he had divulged it to no one during the entire voyage and had even had the series of numbers by which the safe was opened changed when he purchased it in Sydney.

"It seems," explained Simmons, "that by watching you through the keyhole of your cabin, he was able to learn how many turns to the right and left were necessary to open the safe and as for his knowledge of the headdress' value, the shopkeeper where you bought your hatbox in Sydney told him that. It was he, in fact, who bribed Higgins to steal it and bring it back to him, promising to pay him a fancy price for it. If you can remember in which shop you bought the hatbox, we'll have the man arrested when we return to Australia. The disappearance of the other goods you spoke of might be accounted for that way, too. I'll look into it as soon as we land."

"By the way, where are we landing?" asked Mrs. Evans. "I forgot to ask Captain Corcoran."

"I didn't," answered Anita. "We're headed for Apia, Samoa. We can get a boat from there to Honolulu and New York or another from Honolulu to either San Francisco or the way we came, to New York through the Panama Canal, depending on which leaves first."

"You're coming back to the United States with us, of course?" Mrs. Evans asked Mr. Carter as they paused for a moment by the ship's railing to gaze at the sky.

"Of course," he replied. "I've got to deliver the headdress to Mr. Burton and collect for it and then open an office for Simmons and get him started in business."

The journey from Tongareva to Samoa was quickly accomplished and as the little party went ashore at Apia, they found a steamer there, ready to sail for New York within the next few hours. The shops there soon yielded presentable clothes for all, but the girls and Mrs. Evans carefully packed away the sarongs they had worn as well as the headdresses S'fu made for them as treasured reminders of their pleasant stay on the peaceful little island of Tongareva. As soon as she was presentably garbed, Mrs. Evans lost no time in sending a radio message to Mr. Baldwin in New York, as she knew he was greatly concerned over the welfare of herself and the girls, and an hour or so later, aboard the 'Anatole', which was to take the group back to the United States, she received a reply to her message. Hastily tearing open the envelope as the 'Anatole' left Apia on its two thousand, two hundred and sixty mile journey to Honolulu, Mrs. Evans smiled as she read the wire.

MRS. FLORENCE EVANS
ABOARD S.S. ANATOLE
APIA, SAMOA
HOORAY (she read) NOW I CAN SLEEP. HURRY HOME. ALL OAKDALE IS FRANTIC
(signed) BALDWIN.

"I imagine the folks back home are pretty much worried," Alice mused as Mrs. Evans read the message aloud. "They haven't heard from us in almost three months, except for that one message of our safety."

"Let's write to them now," Mabel suggested. "It'll give us something to do at least until we get to Honolulu and we can send the letters home via air mail from there."

"That's a good idea," commended Mrs. Evans. "Each of us can write her own full account of our adventure while it's still fresh in our minds. They'll make very interesting letters to send home as well as supplying accurate information for our Camp Fire records. And that reminds me," she suddenly exclaimed, "I've got to get busy on an official report to Headquarters. They'll want to know about our newest addition to Camp Fire on Tongareva Island, among other things."

"And I expect you'd like to know what happened to my Aunt Minnie and the rest of the crew of the

'Corsair'?" said a voice behind them which the girls at once recognized as Captain Regan's.

"Your Aunt Minnie?" asked Lenore, puzzled. "Who is—- Oh!" she suddenly exclaimed, "you mean Mrs. Crawford! Is she safe? I do hope she's all right."

"She is, thank you," smiled the captain. "I've been sending out radio messages ever since we landed at Apia and just found out that she and the other members of my crew who were in the lifeboat with her, arrived at San Francisco a week ago. They were picked up by a steamer headed in that direction shortly before the storm ceased. She got in touch with Mr. Hunt and he notified her that we, too, were safe. They'll meet us in New York."

"Is Mr. Hunt angry?" asked Mabel as Captain Regan was about to walk away.

"Angry?" he repeated. "Why should he be angry?"

"Well, losing an expensive yacht like the 'Corsair' is nothing to be pleased about, is it?" she replied.

"Oh, that!" laughed Captain Regan. "No, I don't think he'll be angry. To tell the truth, I think he's a little bit pleased, since we're all safe, because now he can build an even bigger and more expensive yacht. That's his hobby, you know."

"Will you be the captain of it?" asked Dolores.

"I'm pretty sure I will be," grinned the captain. "Want to join my crew?"

"I wouldn't mind," smiled Lenore, 'provided you stayed away from typhoons and coral reefs."

"As if I went out looking for that storm and those reefs," mocked the captain.

"Has Mr. Hunt ever been shipwrecked?" asked Anita.

"Several times," replied Captain Regan, "but, just as he will do now, he keeps on building bigger and better yachts, trying to improve on the old ones."

"If he keeps that up," smiled Alice, "he'll have an ocean liner on his hands."

"I hope he does!" laughed Captain Regan boyishly, "because that's the goal I've set for myself, to pilot the biggest ocean liner in the world, some day."

"Well, I hope you get your chance," smiled Dolores, "but when you do, you'd better have Mr. Hunt or whoever owns her, put a special reef finder and typhoon avoider on it for you!"

Busy with letter writing and the compilation of reports for Camp Fire records, the five Camp Fire girls and their leader barely noted the swift passage of time until one day about a week after leaving Apia, they were surprised to see the Hawaiian Islands ahead of them as the 'Anatole' pointed her nose toward beautiful Pearl Harbor and Honolulu. Quickly completing their letters and reports, the girls and Mrs. Evans went ashore, mailed them and strolled about for the hour or so at their disposal before the 'Anatole' sailed again. Looking at familiar scenes and sights was fun for they had been in Honolulu before, when, at the request of National

Camp Fire Headquarters, they had flown around the world in the interests of Camp Fire.

"This is where I'm going to live some day," announced Lenore, clutching the lei around her neck closer to her throat. "No cold winters or sad autumns, just one long springtime all year round. I've half a mind to stay here now and let the rest of you go back by yourselves. I always said if I ever got back here, I'd never leave."

"That's all you ever had, was half a mind," scoffed Mabel. "I'd like to stay here, too, but if we can't, there's no use getting mushy about it. Come on, let's start back or we'll miss the boat and there isn't any sense in that, because there's always another one."

"We'll come back some day," promised Mrs. Evans as a short while later they watched the beautiful islands fade in the distance while the 'Anatole' bore them nearer and nearer to New York and home.

Three weeks later, after a brief visit to Camp Fire Headquarters in New York the five happy girls and their equally delighted leader, sprang from the train at the little railroad station in Oakdale into the eagerly outstretched arms of ten overjoyed parents and one beaming husband while happy laughter and tears made conversation impossible and unnecessary.

"It was a glorious adventure," Anita said later, speaking for the others as well as herself, "and I wouldn't have missed it for worlds, but the best part of it all was coming home again."